Christian's Quest

by Jacqueline Busch & Melvin Patterson

MOODY PUBLISHERS

CHICAGO

Edited by Cynthia Ballenger
Interior and cover design: Design Corps
Cover and interior illustrations: Melvin Patterson
Colorization of cover illustration: John Wollinka/Design Corps
Author Photos: Bob Mead / Photo Press, Inc.

Library of Congress Cataloging-in-Publication Data

Busch, Jacqueline.
    Christian's quest / Jacqueline Busch & Melvin Patterson.
      p. cm.
    Summary: Resets the tale of Little Pilgrim's Progress, portraying Christian as an African American boy who travels from the City of Destruction to the Celestial City through a contemporary urban environment, experiencing physical and spiritual obstacles along the way. Includes discussion questions, glossary, and allegorical key.
    ISBN 978-0-8024-0600-2 (pbk.)
    [1. Christian life--Fiction.] I. Patterson, Melvin. II. Bunyan, John, 1628-1688. Pilgrim's progress. III. Title.
    PZ7.B958Chr 2012
    [Fic]--dc23

                                                                    2012023831

1 3 5 7 9 10 8 6 4 2

Printed in the United States of America

DEDICATIONS

To our King

Thank You for choosing us for this project. We're in awe of You and owe You everything. This is Your story. Use it for Your glory and Yours alone. "Now to Him who is able to do immeasurably more than all we ask or imagine, according to His power that is at work within us, to Him be glory in the church and in Christ Jesus throughout all generations, for ever and ever! Amen." (Ephesians 3:20–21 NIV)

To Glen Kehrein

Thank you for so willingly giving one-hundred and eighty feet of floor to ceiling space to a mural dream and for believing in a God-sized project. We thank God for you. Wish you could tell us what the Celestial City really looks like! Much love to you.

To beloved King's Kids everywhere

This book is for you. Praying that you will come to know and love the good King who created you and loves you with a deep unimaginable love. He has a special purpose for your life. Finish your journey well!

CONTENTS

1

D'CITY

Hey! Yo, Chris! Wait up!" Christian cringed at the sound of Hopeful's voice. It was just a week ago when Hopeful, along with the rest of the Cool Crew, laughed at him because of his feelings. Man, he wanted to be left alone right now. He didn't have time or energy for any more ridicule.

Christian continued walking. He wasn't sure if he had enough patience not to steal on Hopeful and hit him right in his eye. Hopeful, who lived just a few blocks down from Christian, was often two-faced. On his own he was a great guy, but around others he was different. His actions and words became negative and he would make poor choices. Christian's mom said that's what made him a "follower."

"Yo, Chris!" Hopeful yelled in a way that almost seemed like begging. "Chris! Wait up, man! You're not still mad at me, are you?"

Christian turned abruptly. He felt his heart turning as frigid as the January winds now beating against his face. He knew he had to check himself. He didn't have time for confrontation right now. He had somewhere important to go. *Why didn't I remember my gloves?* Christian thought as he stuffed his hands further into the pockets of his bulky Eskimo coat. He wanted to get to his destination—a place, no, a person—where he felt safe, protected, and loved. But he would see what Hopeful wanted and then move on.

"Hey! I need you to . . . to . . . uh . . . uh . . . to . . ." Hopeful bent over, with hands on his knees. His breaths came heavily in and out, the cold wind piercing his lungs from his run making talking difficult.

"Hopeful, what's up?" Christian asked in an icy tone.

"Hey, Chris. I need you to do me a favor."

Christian glanced at him sideways as his heart began to feel weighted. He knew it. A favor. "What kind of favor, man?"

Hopeful looked around nervously and spoke in a low whisper, "I need you to go somewhere with me. I mean . . . us."

"Where and with who?" Suspicion rose in Christian's body and merged with the blasting winter cold. He shivered.

"The Rink with Tina and her cousin Jasmine. I need you to keep Jasi occupied so I can get some alone time with Tina."

Christian grunted. His mind raced. Jasmine was cute, no doubt, but she was also loud and quick to snap off. Besides, pretending to like her would not only be wrong, but would be impossible right now. Playing with her heart a couple of weeks ago would have been easy for Christian, but today his heart and mind were struggling with who he really was. He shivered again.

"So, what's it gonna be? You in?" Hopeful's pleading voice jarred him back to the present.

"Well . . . I don't know. I mean. I was on my way to . . . I . . ." The words all scrambled together and came out in a jumbled mess. A lone burger wrapper floated past him on the sidewalk propelled by the frosty wind. *Oh, to be like that wrapper*, thought Christian. *No hard decisions to make. No peer pressure. No cares in the world.*

"I can't wait all day, man." Hopeful nervously swayed back and forth anticipating a prompt response.

Christian couldn't fight the uneasiness that was rising in the pit of his belly and inching upward. He looked heavenward as if the answer would be written in the sky or someone would instantly give him the courage to say no. Instead a vision flashed in his mind. It was so quick, he thought it never happened. It was the face of the man Christian admired most: his grandfather. His grandfather had the look of a man who could not be swayed. He stood firm on what he believed. Christian drew strength and confidence from this image and knew what he had to do.

"Sorry, Hopeful. I can't. Got some place to go. Somebody's waitin' on me." He looked up to the sky and sighed inwardly. That last part wasn't entirely true. Christian didn't know if his grandfather was home or not. It was a white lie, but a lie nonetheless. His mom always told him that a lie was a lie no matter how big or small it was. He hoped that telling a lie this time would be all right. At least, he meant no harm.

"Man, you ain't no fun. You're becoming a Goody Two-Shoes just like that other girl. What's her name? What,

Oh, to be like that wrapper, thought Christian. No cares in the world.

Faithful? Well, gotta go." And Hopeful shuffled dejectedly, with his head bowed, down the street toward the bus stop.

Christian kicked a wayward pop can on the sidewalk, sending it twisting and spinning, and he walked off in the opposite direction from Hopeful toward his intended destination.

2

GRAMPS

Knock, knock, knock. Christian's knuckles stung as they struck the familiar heavy wooden door, but Christian didn't mind too much. He anxiously listened for the shuffling of feet and the click of the lock. "Please be home," he whispered out loud. Even though it was bitterly cold outside, the door's dark cherry stain and solid construction always filled his heart with warmth and security. It was a reflection of the man who lived inside.

Shuffle, shuffle. Click.

"Hey, Gramps!"

"Chris!" said Gramps as he wrapped him up in a firm yet loving hug. "How ya doin', Son? Come on in out of this cold air. We gotta get you warmed up!"

Christian loved being at his grandfather's house and often visited when he needed to get away from the cries of his little baby sister or when he needed someone to talk to. Today was one of those times.

"Sweet and sour chews?"

Good ol' Gramps, Christian thought as he joyfully chose a handful of the sweet and sour chews. Those sweet and sour sugary treats had a way of making troubles, however large or small, seem not so bad. Gramps seemed to always anticipate Christian's visits with an ample supply of candy treasures stuffed in a brown paper bag.

"Looks like you need to talk, Son. So, what's on your mind today?" Gramps asked as he settled into his favorite brown reclining chair in the living room. Christian breathed a sigh and sat down on the rug next to him. He always wondered how Gramps could read his mind and know when something was bothering him. It felt good to be known and loved that well by someone who loved you unconditionally no matter what choices you made, and someone who always wanted the very best for you. Those people were hard to find these days.

"Gramps, I've been wonderin' . . . ." Christian paused, looking at his grandfather. He didn't know whether or not to go on. What if Gramps thought he was crazy as Hopeful and the Cool Crew did? No matter how many times Christian was laughed at by others, it always stung.

"Go ahead, Son. There's no such thing as a stupid question. The only stupid question is the one that is never asked."

Christian inhaled deeply and continued. "I've been wonderin'. There's got to be more to life than just . . . this. Isn't there?"

Gramps leaned back in his recliner and folded his hands in his lap as a smile slowly crept across his face. Christian stared at his grandfather, waiting in anticipation, and popped another sugary treat in his mouth. His grandfather had a wise face. The wrinkles that were etched all around it were as deep and hard as the thoughts and experiences that shaped his life. Yet somehow, they still reflected his soft endearing heart. Moments seemed like an eternity.

Pop. The instant sour sensation on his tongue did little to calm his pounding heart.

Looking directly at Christian with a gleam in his eye, Gramps answered in a strong, steady voice, "There is more, Christian. Much more."

Christian focused on his grandfather, not wanting to miss a single word. He had learned over the years that when Gramps got "that look," enlightening words would follow and Christian wanted to hear every one.

"There is a beautiful country more awesome than you or I can imagine far away from this city. The Celestial City, it's called. Its streets are built of pure gold with mansions scattered with jewels. There is no pain in this city. No, Chris. No pain. No tears. No hurt or injustice. It's a big praise party where everybody is singin' and playin' all day and night. A good, wise, and all-knowing King rules over it. He loves everyone very much with a love that we can't even imagine."

Christian had a difficult time trying to fathom a love that was greater than his grandfather's love toward him. "So, if that place is so great, then why . . . ." Christian popped another sugary candy in his mouth, hoping it would give him the strength to continue. "Why do we live here in this city?"

"You know, Son," Gramps continued, his voice changing slightly to a more stern tone. "Our city hasn't always been this way. I remember the time when it was so beautiful here. The sun shone brighter in those days. Its rays danced onto grass so green, that you knew it had to be painted by the King Himself, and the streets were clean enough to eat off of. Yes, sir. The people were kinder then."

"So what happened? How did this city become what it is today?" Christian asked, hardly believing the picture his grandfather painted, but knew it had to be the truth. His heart began to yearn for what was in the past.

"Well, Son. This city is called the City of Destruction, D'City for short. We are born here to live our lives as a test of our love and faith to the King. It is His will that we would all one day spend eternity with Him in the Celestial City. But His way of life is different from our own, and instead of forcing us to live His way, He is kind enough to allow us to make a choice to live either for Him or the Wicked Prince."

"Who's the Prince?" Christian asked, hungry for the knowledge Gramps was feeding him. Another Sour Patch exploded on his tongue.

"Well, you see, he was once one of the King's favorite soldiers, but he fell from the King's favor because he desired, most of all, to have power. You see, he thought himself equal to the King and attempted to take what was not his to take.

The King defeated him easily and exiled him to this land where this city now stands. Ever since then, the Prince turned cruel with a deep hatred toward the King and anything belongin' to Him. He doesn't care about people, only that they stay away from the Celestial City like him."

"So, because the Wicked Prince can never get back into the Celestial City, he's hatin' on the King and His people?"

"You got it. Because we are favored by the King, the Wicked Prince has slowly closed people's hearts and minds to our original purpose of loving and serving the King. He's clever and cunning, blinding us to the King's ways to make us serve him instead; tempting us daily with the things we want most to keep us away from the King. So, when we choose to foolishly chase after what we want most (which in many cases is not what the King wants for us), we allow the Wicked Prince to gain power over us. One day, though, the King will send His army to this city to fight the Wicked Prince and his army. This city will be destroyed and all those following the Wicked Prince will die."

"How do you know all this, Gramps?" Another burst of sour, then sweet, flavors filled Christian's mouth. He remembered hearing stories like this being screamed by preachers standing on the city street corners every now and then. Their "gloom and doom" words made him feel condemned like he was so horrible that the King would not let him within ten miles of the Celestial City. Gramps, however, made the King sound awesome like Someone he should get to know.

A look of relief and joy overtook Gramps' face as he pointed to the thick black Book with golden pages, now worn with age, sitting on the coffee table. "From the greatest Book ever written given to us by the King Himself. Oh, it's no story, Son. It's real. Yes, it's real. The King is real."

Christian's mind was now racing. *Is a battle coming, with fire raining down from the sky?* "Gramps, just to be sure, is there any way to escape the battle?" Christian thought of the war video games he played. That was scary enough and that was just a game. He couldn't imagine a real battle with an enormous army and consuming flames. He shivered.

Gramps sat up, leaned forward, and looked intently at Chris. "Sure, my son. Everyone on the King's team is safe. The King keeps His own protected from the Wicked Prince. But, as I said before, He doesn't force you to be on His team. Each person must choose for themselves. Actually..." Gramps paused and glanced across the room at the well-used bookshelf brimming with books of all shapes and sizes. "See that small black book on the second shelf? The one with gold letters on the edge? Go and get it."

Christian walked over and took the book from its place.

"It's time that you read the story for yourself and learn about the King. Take it and read it. It's yours. Now run on

home to your mama. It's gettin' late. And remember, the King loves you even more than I do."

"Thanks, Gramps! Love you too!"

Christian put the Book under his arm, hugged his grandfather, and ran home. Somehow, it didn't feel as cold outside.

3

THE END ZONE

"**H**ut one!"

"Hut two! Hut, hut!"

Hopeful yelled his hard counts with a false sense of urgency. He was attempting to draw the defensive line offside once more. It didn't work this time. He quickly scanned the opposing team's formation. *Zone defense. Good!* Hopeful double tapped his left leg and paused.

That's the signal! Time for me to do what I do! Christian's heart pounded so hard that he could barely hear the cheers coming from the crowd all around him. *Wait for it.* His legs trembled with energy as he imagined himself transformed into a Shelby Mustang. The sound of each breath he released rumbled in unison with his increasing heart rate. He could feel the 500 horsepower of the Shelby's engine revving inside his chest with the promise of insane speed. Hopeful now had but one more word to yell that would set him free.

"Hike!"

Finally! Christian thought as he exploded from his three-point stance. He dashed forward with so much power that he almost ripped Hopeful's arms right off as he received the handoff. The clash of helmets resonated with a thunderous echo in his ears as his teammates dominated the line of scrimmage, opening a hole wide enough to drive a tank through.

Only twenty-four yards until the end zone. I got this, Christian thought as he blew past the middle linebacker, spinning instinctively causing the free safety to miss tackling him. The safety fell on his face in an almost humorous way. *Sucka!* Amused, Christian made his cut for the sidelines. *Now it's just me and the defensive back. He's weak. I'll drop my shoulder and run right over him.*

Christian lived for these moments. He started playing football in an attempt to free his mind from his troubles two years ago. Now he needed football as surely as he needed air to breathe. He had found his niche. He was born to run the football. Football gave him focus, discipline, and made him feel good about himself. Besides giving him purpose, the game gave him weekly opportunities to stand out and be a hero—destroying the confidence of opposing teams each time he kneeled inside the end zone for a touchdown.

The defensive back's eyes widened with nervous anxiety as he prepared for the inevitable collision. He braced himself, but lowered his shoulders too soon before Christian reached him. *Change of plans.* Christian cut to the right, at the same time switching the ball to his right hand and extending his left arm. Giggling, he stiff-armed his opponent to the ground so hard that his face mask filled with grass.

Touchdown!! Christian dropped to one knee, the horn blowing loudly, signaling the end of the game. The fans in the stands were ecstatic, yelling wildly and chanting his name.

We win again! Thanks, King! State champs again. Two years in a row. It doesn't get any better than this.

Coach Reed ran to Christian, embracing him in a big bear hug. Slapping his shoulder pads, Coach Reed yelled, "You're a shoo-in for the MVP, Chris. I'm proud of you, Son. You've made your hometown proud today." Christian's heart slowed as joy flooded in, replacing his adrenaline rush. He closed his eyes and reveled in the cheers and adoration of his loyal fans who loved him because of his unmatched skills.

This is the best day ever, he thought, as the Commissioner of the Scholastic League announced that he, Christian, was voted this year's MVP. *Yes, sir! Nothing can ruin this day,* he thought. Just as Christian started to raise his trophy, his mom came into view. He had almost forgotten she was there. He was so hyped right now from all that he had worked so hard to achieve, that he simply just forgot about her. He smiled at her with pride and joy. She simply smiled back softly, then looked away. *Something's wrong,* Christian thought. He suddenly felt selfish and ashamed. He hoped he hadn't offended her by not acknowledging her immediately after the game. After all, his mom had always been there for him, especially his big games. After handing the trophy to Coach Reed, Christian ran to give his mother a hug.

"We did it, Mom! We did it!"

"I know, Son. I'm so proud of you," she responded softly.

Something is definitely wrong. "Mom, what's up?"

"I had to leave during the game, Chris. I'm sorry, Baby. I didn't even get to see your last touchdown."

"That's okay, Mom." Christian looked deeply into his mom's eyes praying that what was behind them was not disappointment. She attempted to smile but as she gazed back into his eyes, tears began to trickle down her cheeks. She pulled Christian in close and held him so tight that he could feel her shivering. Leaning down she whispered, "Gramps is gone, Baby. Gramps is gone to be with the King."

This had just become the worst day ever.

4

THE BOOK

They did a really good job with Clarence's body."

"Yeah, he really looked good."

"He sho' did! And peaceful."

"How is Chris handlin' all this, Doris?"

"Well, as good as anyone who . . ."

As Christian's mother began to respond to what seemed to be a ridiculous question to his mind, Christian scurried away from the crowd of family and friends who gathered at his home to honor his grandfather's memory. *How can people be so, so silly?* he thought as he ascended the carpeted staircase that led to his sanctuary.

Gramps didn't look good. He looked dead! He is dead! He'd gone away from all these silly people, with their silly thoughts and opinions. He'd gone away from this stupid city. And he'd gone away from him.

How am I supposed to be doing!? No matter how hard he tried to appear strong or attempt to understand the departure of his closest friend, Christian couldn't let go of the overwhelming feelings of sadness, shame, guilt, and regret now digging deeper into the very core of who he was.

He looked around his room and surveyed all the trophies and plaques he had received from playing football for the past two years—symbols of excellence and glory for all that he had achieved. It always made him feel good when he would look at his self-made shrine. Tonight though, he could find no peace in it. Tonight, all this stuff was just a symbol of his selfish pride.

It was because of his lust for fame and glory that those weekly visits with Gramps became monthly visits. The more people who looked up to him and pumped up his ego, the harder he worked to receive their praise. The praise of others became addicting, moreso than any other thing. Never in his life had he been so liked and appreciated. So he decided to work harder still, even if it meant spending less time with those he loved, including Gramps. Soon the monthly visits dwindled down to hardly any, especially this year. Sure, he would see Gramps on birthdays and all other family holidays, but that was it. He had abandoned his love for his grandfather for the love of the game. Football, it seemed, had become his master.

"Well, look a here, look a here! My grandson has become a neighborhood celebrity. I'm so proud of you, Chris! I knew if you really worked hard and applied yourself, you would be one of the best running backs ever. I was quite the football player back in my day too, ya know. Yes, sir! People used to call me The Rocket cuz of the fire trailin' me as I shot down field for touchdown after touchdown." Gramps smiled widely and looked deeply into Christian's eyes before continuing. "Don't you worry 'bout me and the visits, Son. You just keep on practicing so you become better and better. See me when

you can. I have lived my life, Chris. Now you gotta live yours. Just don't forget about the King. He gave you the gift you have. I'll see you at the games. You know I'm comin' to as many games as this old body will allow. I'll be cheerin' you on with everything I got! I love you, Chris. Never forget that either!"

"I love you too, Gramps."

Good ol' Gramps. That conversation was a year and a half ago. Tears began to run down Christian's face. He could hold them back no longer. Christian knew Gramps was only saying those things to him so that he wouldn't feel guilty. He knew that he should've given a little less time to football and a little more time to Gramps. *Why didn't I? Gramps always seemed to be there for me. From the most serious to the downright silliest problems I faced, Gramps always made time for me! Why didn't I do the same for him?*

Christian sobbed uncontrollably now. Anger began to replace regret as he wrestled with himself. Who would be there for him now? Where would he find the answers to life's challenges that lay before him?

Gramps always talked about going home to be with the King. In fact, he looked forward to it. No more worries. No more crying. No more struggling to deal with the pressures of this life of captivity, chained to the harsh realities that the City of Destruction was all too willing to dish out daily. Gramps was free and with the King.

Christian ran over to the dresser that supported most of his trophies with every intention of knocking them all down when . . .

"Why are you acting like this, Son? You don't have to be angry. Let it go. I loved you because the King first loved me. You still got the Book. Any wisdom that you feel you got from me, I got straight from the words found in that Book. Read it and you will find your way. I love you, Chris—now and forever!"

The voice stopped him dead in his tracks.

"Gramps." Christian struggled to grasp what just happened. He knew he heard his grandfather speaking to him, giving him advice and leading him in the right direction as always. He had heard him clear as day. But how? Gramps was dead. Wasn't he?

"Gramps?" Christian called out once more. His anger was now replaced with fear and wonder. If it really was his grandfather talking to him then it would mean he was a ghost. Don't be silly! Christian redirected his attention to finding the Book his grandfather had given to him two years ago.

Where was it? He checked the top of his dresser, the closet, and in his box where he kept his most coveted comic books. Not there. He started dumping the clothes found in the drawers of his dresser. Not there. He then began to frantically toss the few books he held in the small bookcase next to the desk where he did his homework. Not there either. *Where did I put that Book?! If I lost that Book I would never forgive myself!* He shut his eyes tightly in an attempt to calm himself. Think, Christian! Be still and think! He had heard his grandfather say this to himself whenever he couldn't find what he was looking for. It always worked for him. Just maybe . . .

Christian opened his eyes and smiled. The Book was on his nightstand to the right of his bed, where it always was. He put it there as a reminder to read it daily before going to sleep. That too was lost because of his love for football. *I really hope the King does forgive us for our wrong choices in the past, present, and future.* He picked it up and wiped the thick layer of dust from its cover. The gold paint used to fill in the title letters glowed extremely bright in contrast to the deep black dye used for the leather bound cover.

Christian thought that he had lost his grandfather forever. Now he understood that Gramps was still with him in a way. Through the words contained in this Book, Gramps would still be guiding him because this was the map that guided Gramps. Christian let out a sigh of relief, then returned to mingle with the guests downstairs. He felt better now that he let go of some of the sadness of Gramps being gone. The guilt was still there, but he knew that his grandfather didn't hold his actions against him. Why else would Gramps interrupt his rest to give Christian direction? Gramps was cool with Christian playing football and loved him.

Thanks, King, for letting Gramps talk to me one last time. Because of his earlier talks about the Book with his grandfather he knew that if he lived his life the King's way that he would see Gramps again in the Celestial City. That thought filled his heart with joy as he began to pile loads of food on his plate. What a feast they'd been blessed with! It was like an early Thanksgiving given in honor of his grandfather.

After all the festivities had ended and everyone returned to their own homes, Christian talked to the King about his entire family. And even though he didn't read it that night, he found comfort in the Book by just holding it close to his heart as he slept.

Thanks, Gramps, for all you have done for me. I'll miss you and I love you. Now and forever!

5
CONFRONTATION

The sound of whizzing cars and water cascading from the nearby fountain blended together to create a busy, yet relaxing, melody at Destruction Park. Christian loved to come here and read the Book. Even though this melody played somewhat loudly, the rushing of metal and water created a kind of force field around him that drowned out distracting sounds.

It had been a few months since he started to again read the book his Gramps had given him. The stories of the King and His promises to all who choose to follow him excited and confused Christian at the same time.

How could the King love someone like him? Everything the King considered to be wrong, Christian either enjoyed doing or couldn't wait to be old enough to do: drinking, parties, chasing girls, fighting, roastin' fools, telling jokes about people, and even his love for football, because he loved it more than anything. *Maaan! That's crazy! How am I gonna be able to give up football? And am I really supposed to love the King more than my mama?!*

Christian's frustration still couldn't sway his heart from yearning to experience the peace that came from being a part of the King's family. He imagined himself in the Celestial City chillin, for all eternity with Gramps and the King. No more cryin'. No more children gettin' shot in the streets. Nobody breakin' into houses and stealin' stuff and everyone living together in harmony as one. *Now that would be nice!*

The King has to have a football league! Why else would He have made me so good? I'm gonna play on His team when I get to the Celestial City for sure! This made Christian smile as he ended his reading session for the day.

As Christian was readying himself to leave, he saw the members of his old crew, the Cool Crew, entering the park to hang out. He was happy to see them. This was a great chance for him to share all that he had learned about the King and His promises. If he could get them to see the importance of joining the King as he did, then they would be saved from the coming battle as well. *Chillin' in the house of the King together would be a wonderful thing. Wouldn't it?*

"Hey yo! Guys! Wait up!" Christian yelled as he quickened his strut in order to join his friends.

"What up, Chris?" asked Obstinate as he extended his hand for the Cool Crew handshake.

"Nothin' much, O'. Just hangin' low and lettin' knowledge be born." They ended with their left arms around each other as their right hands remained clutched together in the front of them. It was a false sign of unity.

"For real, Joe?" asked Pliable as he now stepped forward to continue their ritualistic greeting.

"For real, Joe!" replied Christian.

"Knowledge 'bout what?" asked Pliable who seemed genuinely interested. After Christian completed his greetings with the other members of the crew, he began to tell them about what he had been reading.

"Oh please! That's not knowledge! That's garbage, man!" yelled Obstinate in a very agitated tone. "You expect us to stop everything that we love doin' because of the junk you read in that old book? Maaan, you're crazy!" Obstinate waved his hands as if to shoo Christian away.

"Yeah, Chris. I mean, if this King was so good, why would He come to kill us? We didn't do anything to Him! You sure you not readin' some crazy serial killer's book? You know they like to start cults, man!"

The rest of the group started laughing at the statements being hurled so sarcastically by Pliable. "Man, this dude is crazy!"

"Yeah, man! Crazy Chris!" yelled another of his crew members as the laughter escalated from low to hysterical at this new tag name that would now become Christian's new label.

"I'm not crazy! I got this Book from my grandfather and he told me that this stuff was going to happen!" Christian's arm was lifting with power and focus before he even finished his statement. His fist landed too fast for Obstinate to react. It was a crushing blow, full of the anger and rage that was fueled by this unnecessary roastin'. Christian hit Obstinate in the jaw so hard, that it sounded like he might have broken it. That was all it took to silence the crowd.

"Gramps was a good man. Smarter than anyone I ever knew." Christian pointed a shaky finger toward Obstinate before continuing. "How many times did you get money, food, and other stuff from him? I dare you to try to roast Gramps!" Christian, with both fists now closed tightly, raised his arms slowly and turned to the rest of guys. "I double dare you to call Gramps a liar and most importantly . . . I dare any one of you to call my King a liar!" Christian stood his ground ready to take on anyone brave enough to come forward.

Obstinate managed to get to his feet. He was the toughest of the Cool Crew, tougher than Christian ever was. In a heads up, one-on-one fight Obstinate knew he could kick Christian's butt in a heartbeat, but that punch caught him off guard. Shaking his head in an attempt to regain all his senses, he motioned for the rest of the crew not to make a move on Christian.

"That was the hardest punch I ever got from a little punk like you. I should kick yo' lil' butt . . ." Obstinate paused in order to let the pain in his jaw lessen just a bit before continuing. "But because you just lost your grandfather . . . a man who . . . , as you said, was very nice to me, I'm gonna let this one slide.

"But, Crazy Chris, listen up! Don't come around us again unless you are ready to hang out or get banged up! Cuz we don't want to hear that garbage again! We don't care about

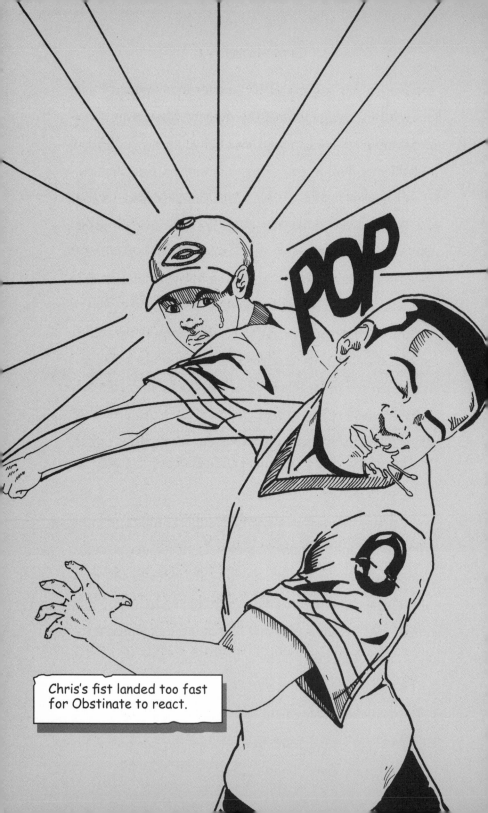

Chris's fist landed too fast for Obstinate to react.

the King or His stupid rules! And after today we don't care about you! Now get outta here before I change my mind!" Obstinate glared at Christian hoping that he would still want to fight.

Tears now flowed down Christian's face like the water cascading from the fountain about forty yards from this confrontational standoff. He knew that there was no way he could really beat Obstinate in a fair fight. Besides, even if he could win, how would that be displaying the King's love? No! It's better to accept the grace given by Obstinate and go home.

Christian, with his head bowed, began to walk home. Obstinate had defeated him without throwing a punch. The Cool Crew began to cheer for their leader wildly. "Hey!" Christian yelled firmly at the crowd of young men. His bold tone caused them to stop jocking Obstinate and returned their attention to him for just a moment.

"What, Fool?" yelled Obstinate as the others stood in silent amazement. Christian had courage. No doubt!

"I care about all of you . . . and the King cares about all of you even more than I do!" As these words left Christian's mouth, he no longer felt defeated. And even though he continued to cry for his friends, he now walked away with his head held high.

6

DIRECTION

The soft glow of pulsating blue light coming from the top of the surveillance box seemed to hypnotize Christian more and more with every flicker of its alluring light. *If D' City is so great, why do we need these stupid boxes?* Christian thought to himself as he refocused on his need to get home. Looking upward, he glanced down the street to the left, then to the right. Christian could see several of these boxes attached to the top of random streetlight poles. The Wicked Prince ordered them to be installed to supposedly make the citizens of the city feel safer.

"Get that fool, D!" yelled a guy wearing a red jersey and red baseball cap tilted to the left side.

Christian jerked around just in time to see a very large, yet nimble, guy grab a similarly built man by the hood of his blue sweatshirt. D's strength, combined with the other guy's momentum, created enough force to pull the unlucky guy backwards and off his feet. He hadn't even hit the ground before a group of five or six guys surrounded him and began to give him a serious beat-down.

Looking away from the flurry of punches and kicks for a moment, Christian stared in amazement at all the grownups standing around, watching silently, and doing nothing except pointing fingers and shaking their heads. They were too afraid of retaliation to even tell the young men to stop.

"Hey . . . guys! That's enough!" said a man with a very large afro, black shades, and dressed in beige and blue. "I said . . . that's enough!" He spoke with authority and without fear. The young men, now out of breath from the continuous punching and kicking, turned to face this courageous man. They had every intention of attacking him next. That is, until they realized who it was.

"Help. Uh . . . hey, man! Sorry. Uh, we didn't hear you comin'. We're done whoopin' this fool anyway," said the guy who yelled at D. "We were mindin' our business when this Cat came up and started dissin' our gang. You know we can't allow that, Help. People'll start believin' the Lords are soft." His voice went from deep to almost whiny as he pleaded his case.

"Okay, Tim. I really don't care why or how it started. I just want it to stop. Ya dig? If you guys are so tough, how come you didn't fight the Cat heads up? Now step!" Help had already placed himself between the Lords and the poor member of the Cats. He stood firm, strong arms folded across a broad chest, without worry or fear of retaliation.

Tim, D, and the rest of the Lords just backed away without a word being said. Nobody messed with Help. Nobody! He was a street legend. He beat up more gang leaders and thugs than anyone in D' City. It was even rumored that he took on twelve members of one gang all alone, and he won! *Man, to be like him!* Christian thought as he looked upward to see a surveillance box right above the scene of the crime.

These boxes are useless! Christian suddenly felt very sad. Tears began to roll down his cheeks again. He turned to walk away from yet one more reason why it would be so much better to leave D'City.

I can't believe I used to think this place was so great. How could we all be so blinded to the realities of living here? Christian's heart began to feel heavier as he slowly walked down the street. Everyone and everything in D'City looked so different to him now. He had played up and down these streets all of his life. The concrete slabs of the sidewalk, the bricks of the buildings, and the people who seemed to have nothing else to do but hang out in the exact same spots day after day all now seemed foreign to him.

Christian came to a halt at the changing of the streetlight and the rush of cars now hurrying past the intersection. He stood patiently and watched all the people around him. *How can they not know, or maybe not care about the battle to come? Are they all blinded by the Wicked Prince's tricks, unable to see that this place is really a prison? Why can't they see what I see?*

Just as the streetlight changed to green, Christian caught the sounds of an organ playing and a choir singing. Normally he would just keep on walking, but his ears also picked up a voice in the background of all that noise. Instead of crossing the street, Christian now turned in the direction of the faint, yet powerful, voice. "The King gave this promise to everyone" . . . Christian's pace quickened as the voice began to get louder and more understandable. ". . . That anyone who believeth in Him shall be saved! Say Amen, somebody!"

"Amen!" shouted most of the people in the crowd at the request of this strong and authoritative voice. Amen! thought Christian as he hurried through the very tall wooden doors surrounded by a white stone and massive concrete structure. The voice led him to a church where its owner, a short, stocky bald minister, was giving a moving and exciting sermon on the promises of the King. His every word was electrifying. The emotional charge of the congregation increased as he began to hammer the promises of the King home.

This guy is awesome! He sounds just like Gramps but with more power! Christian's heart was now pounding so hard he thought it would jump right out of his chest! *This guy can help me! I'm not leaving until I talk to him!*

Christian had to wait for the service to end and for the people to leave, but he didn't mind. His need to talk to this teacher of the Word was now more important than anything. As he approached this minister of hope, Christian was totally set at ease by the soft and kind features of the man's face and his gentle way of talking with people. *Yes sir! This is definitely the man to talk to!*

"Excuse me, Sir. Thank you for your sermon." Christian said as he extended his right hand. The minister's extended hand caught Christian's midway and they began the up and down motion that completed the customary greeting.

"Now that's a firm grip, young man!" said the minister whose smile seemed to widen as he spoke.

"Thank you! I get that from my grandfather." Christian smiled. "Gramps always told me that a man gains respect by shaking hands firmly while looking the other person directly in the eyes."

"Gramps sounds like a very wise man. I like to look in the eyes of people I meet too! Shows me their character. Sure does! You can tell a lot about a man from lookin' him in the eyes." The minister paused to scan Christian with a piercing gaze. "Your eyes are tellin' me that you got a lot on your mind and even though you seem to be at ease for the moment, your eyes have been rainin' tears pretty recently, correct?"

Christian simply nodded and answered "Yes, Sir."

"Sir?" The minister's face shriveled from this show of respect. Christian silently hoped he had not offended him. "No need for such formal titles, Son. M' name is Evangelist. I can tell that you are here concernin' the King. And since I have been walkin' in the way of the King since I was old enough to read . . ." Evangelist smiled, grabbed Christian by the shoulder, and guided him to the closest seat available before continuing. "Let's see if I can give you the answers you are looking for. Now before we begin, what's your name, Son?"

"Christian, but my friends call me Chris."

"Well, Chris. Can I call you Chris?" Christian happily nodded. "Let's see if I can answer your questions."

Evangelist talked to Christian for about two hours. He told Christian with great certainty that the stories found in the Book were all true. From cover to cover, the Book was written to give hope to the hopeless, to give guidance to the lost and, most importantly, the Book was a reminder of the King's undying love for all people. "No matter who you are or what you may have done in your past, Chris, know that the King loves you . . . and if you accept Him there will be a place for you in His kingdom forever."

"The Celestial City!" Christian blurted with excitement. This seemed to make Evangelist smile wider than ever before.

"Yes, Chris. The Celestial City." Evangelist's eyes began to glisten as he described this wonderful place. White buildings that towered into the bluest skies, built atop streets of the purest gold, and surrounded entirely by the glow from the glory of the King's majesty. Christian could hardly contain himself. He had to get to the Celestial City and he had to get there pronto!

"Can you show me the way?" Christian nearly screamed. His eyes were popping with excitement and he felt his own smile widen to almost match Evangelist.

This was a question that Evangelist had not expected. He stared deeply into Christian's eyes and released a heavy sigh. "Chris, you sure about this? Because you gotta be sure! The way is easily seen for those who want it bad enough and I can see you do. But many adults have attempted this journey and failed. I can only imagine how hard the Wicked Prince is going to make this trip for one as young as you. You see, the Wicked Prince hates to lose anyone who was born under his reign."

"Please, Evangelist. I want . . . NO! I *need* this more than anything!" Christian cried in desperation. The dam that held back his earlier tears now gave way to new ones.

"I hope so, for your sake, Chris." Evangelist stood up. "Follow me." He led Christian back outside the two massive wood doors, pointing eastward before reconnecting his gaze with Christian. "You see that light shining up yonder?" Christian squinted for a moment before a tiny twinkle of light caught his eye.

"Yes," he answered.

"That's where you're headed. Once there you will pass through the Shepherd's Gate that separates the Wicked Prince's land from the King's way. Be careful, Chris, for the Wicked Prince will stop at nothing to keep you from

"You see that light shining up yonder? That's where you're headed."

reconnecting with the King. When you find yourself weak or needing help, call on the King and He will give you what you need to endure." The smile that was once pasted on Evangelist's face now returned and before Christian knew it, he was wrapped up in a joyful embrace. "May the King keep you covered in His everlasting grace and protection!"

"Thank you, Evangelist!" Christian waved goodbye as he turned to run home to prepare for this trip of a lifetime.

7

THE SACK

"**H**ave courage, Chris!**"** He was excited for the journey, but at the same time he was still uncertain what he would face along the way. *I would feel so much better if I didn't have to do this alone!* Even though D'City was his home since birth, he knew in his heart he no longer belonged there. He had to get away from this place. Christian walked past the abandoned lot where he used to chill out with his friends, past the corner store where he used to buy his favorite sweet and sour chews, and past the hot dog stand where he bought the best tasting hot dogs ever made. But none of this could distract him from his chosen path. Christian was on a mission and his mind was made up. He needed a different life and he desperately wanted to meet the King. He began to run.

His running soon turned into a slow jog, however, and then a fast-paced walk. He stopped and bent over gasping for breath, his hands resting on his thighs. "Ugh, I hate this burden!" In his eager haste to begin his journey, Christian forgot all about it. Other people couldn't see it, but he could feel the weight of it and he hated the way it hindered his movements.

His mind flashed back to a conversation he had with Evangelist the day after he discovered the burgundy sack tied securely on his back.

"It is common," Evangelist had begun, "for all those who truly accept the King and His ways to receive a sack that represents the burden of bad choices made in the past and present. Some of the sacks are larger than others. Now you must be sure, Chris, to follow the King's ways and don't make the same wrong choices, and you'll be all right. The more wrong choices you make, the heavier the burden becomes. But don't worry. The sack will be removed once you arrive at the Place of the Cross."

Christian had been relieved to hear that the sack would only be a temporary nuisance, but now he winced as he suffered from one more reason why he had to travel the King's Path. His hands still stung from his vain attempts of trying to remove the burden himself, as he had quickly and painfully discovered the rope could not be torn, cut, nor burned. He had to get rid of this sack!

Tears swelled in Christian's eyes as he trudged on, one foot in front of the other, in the direction that Evangelist had pointed him. He longed for his mom's reassuring touch. She always knew how to encourage him. *Mama.* His mind flooded with images of his mom, her love, her tender words, her look of confusion as she tried desperately to understand why he was going on this journey alone away from her and away from his baby sister who was just starting to walk.

The tears threatened to spill down his cheeks, but Christian blinked them away. His mind was made up. No use looking back now. He had to go. He knew it. Nothing, no one could hold him back. He had to be strong; no use being a punk about it. His mom and sister would be fine. Didn't Gramps say that the King watched over everyone?

"Yo, Chris! Hold up, man!" Christian thought he was imagining a voice shouting out his name. *Naw, it can't be. Didn't see anybody comin' this way. Besides, I'm not stoppin' for nobody!* He forced his legs to move faster, doing his best to fight against the load that was pressing hard on his back and legs.

"Chris! Chris! Hey, wait up!"

Christian heard the voice again accompanied by footsteps approaching fast and knew then it was not his imagination. His steps quickened with his heartbeat, but his burden pressed in, causing him to stumble down beneath its oppressing weight. Thud. His shoulder hit the ground. Hard. He looked up in surprise to see a familiar face peering over him.

"Hey, Chris! Where you goin', man?"

Two sweaty hands reached out to help him to his feet, as he sighed inwardly. *Pliable.*

Christian stood up tall, gripping the Book tighter in an effort to gain the courage that had quickly left him. "I'm going to the Celestial City to the King. Wanna come with?"

"Uh, hey. I've been thinkin'. What if you are right?" Pliable's voice came softly, as he glanced around nervously. "I think I'm goin' to go with you."

A look of shock and surprise came over Christian's face. "You sure?"

"Sure. I'll try it."

Christian put his hand on Pliable's shoulder. "You have to believe in the King and want to follow Him. C'mon, then. Let's go!" Suddenly Christian's burden didn't seem so heavy anymore. The King provided him a companion to walk and talk with.

8

DEAD MAN'S SWAMP

"So, Chris," Pliable began. "You really sure that Book of yours is true? I don't wanna be goin' to some fantasy place that doesn't exist."

"Yep!" Christian replied. "I'm 100 percent sure. It's written by the King who cannot lie. There really IS a place called the Celestial City. For real!"

"So tell me what this Celestial City is like."

And so as they walked on together, Christian excitedly described the Celestial City.

Pliable stopped in his tracks and turned to Christian. "For real? You mean that's the place where we are headin' now? How do we get there?" Pliable's voice shook with excitement.

"Evangelist told me that we have to go through the Shepherd's Gate first. It's this way. We gotta follow that twinkling light. See it in the distance?"

Pliable squinted, but his mind was somewhere else. "Man, I can't wait to see my mansion! It'll be tight! Oohh . . . imagine me chillin' out in my crib with diamonds all around! C'mon, Chris! Let's walk faster!" And with that, Pliable grabbed Christian's arm pulling him to go faster.

"Hold up, Pliable! I can't go that fast cuz of this weight! Slow down!" As Christian yanked his arm away, struggling under the weight of his oppressive sack, a quiet but distinct voice hissed disturbing thoughts in his ear. *You'll never make it that far, not with all the wrong choices you've made. You think the King will want you? You are so dumb. You left your mom and sister for this? Who do you think you are?*

"Man, I'm so happy I came with you." Pliable's voice interrupted Christian's thoughts. "Man, if this journey to the King is this easy . . ."

"What the . . .!" Pliable shrieked. He and Christian were so focused on their conversation that they weren't watching where they were going. A dark brown goop that reeked of filth encircled their feet and lower legs. Holding his nose, Pliable shouted, "Man, my new shoes are ruined! I didn't come here for this! Crazy Chris, get me out of here!"

Although he barely moved, Christian found himself sinking farther and farther into the soft muddy ground. *What is this stuff?* he wondered. Evangelist warned him of troubles, but he didn't remember him saying anything about this mud pit that was now threatening to entrap him and Pliable in its muddy prison.

Christian glanced over to see Pliable struggling in the mud, hollering at the top of his lungs. "I said get me out of here, Chris! Man, I can't believe I trusted you! You so stupid." After several desperate attempts to free himself from the filth that was surrounding him, Pliable managed to regain his footing with the help of a solid branch and pulled himself out, smeared in the goop from head to toe. "You know what? I'm gone, Crazy Chris. If this is what your journey is like to the stupid golden city, you can have it! I'm goin' home. See ya!" And with a mocking wave of his hand, Pliable trudged away, continuing to yell insults. All hope Christian had faded with Pliable's image into the distance.

Christian suddenly felt alone and panic began to overwhelm him. He thrashed about vigorously in the knee-deep sludge trying to gain a foothold, but lost his footing and choked on the muddy goop. The foul stench filled his nostrils and he gagged. The more he struggled, the more he sank into the slough because of the heavy burden on his back. Christian started to tremble uncontrollably, tears streaming down his face, as he began to surrender to his gloomy stinky demise. "What have I done? Oh, King, what have I done? King, help me!"

No sooner had the desperate words left his lips did Christian hear a voice. At first, he thought he was imagining it. But, then he heard it again. A strong, steady voice.

"Chris, I'm here. Over here. I'm here to help you."

Christian glanced over his mud-covered shoulder toward the direction of The Shepherd's Gate and gasped. There stood Help. The dude he remembered seeing in D'City, the Legend himself. He still wore that large afro and black shades.

"Here, catch this rope." Christian strained forward with all his might to catch the lifeline that landed squarely in front of him and grabbed on tightly.

With swift, strong pulls, Help drew Christian out of the foul, muddy slough and set him on firm solid ground. Christian stood, his entire body shaking, encrusted with gooey, stinky mud.

"How did you get in there? Didn't you see the stepping stones?" Help asked quietly, with obvious patience in his voice.

His head down, Christian answered, "I . . . I . . . guess I was too busy talking and not paying attention. What is this place anyway?"

"You gotta watch where you are going. This is the Slough of Despond, but most people call it Dead Man's Swamp. People fall into it when they feel like they aren't good enough or let the fear overtake them. Many die here tryin' to get out on their own."

"That's why it's called Dead Man's Swamp." Christian gulped, silently thankful that was not his fate.

Help nodded. "The only way out is with the King's help. He sent me to pull you out. In the future, Chris, make sure you watch for the King's Path and follow it closely."

"I will." Filled with shame and embarrassment from his clumsiness and his foul odor, Christian forced himself to look into the eyes of the man who saved his life. "Thank you." "You are welcome, Chris. You are loved by the King. Now go on. Walk toward the light, trust in the King, and all will be well."

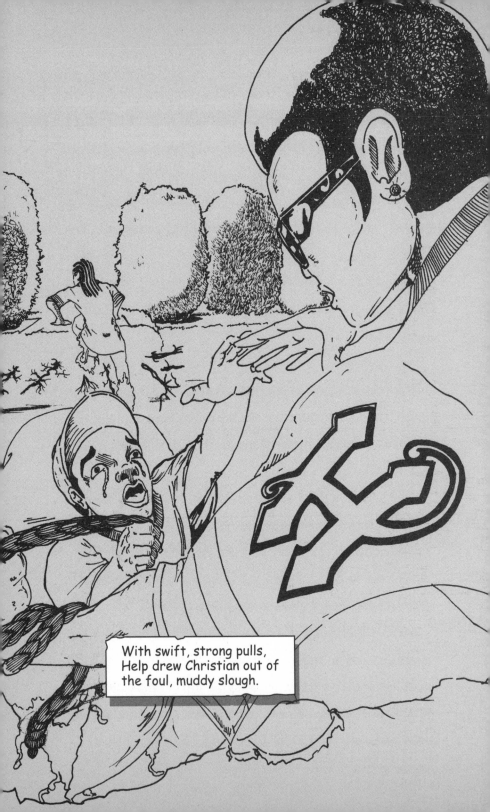

With swift, strong pulls, Help drew Christian out of the foul, muddy slough.

And with that, Christian lifted his eyes, hefted the sack to a more bearable position on his back, and breathed in a big breath of courage. Doing his best to ignore the foul stench and mud that engulfed him, he began to walk toward the twinkling light in the distance.

9

DOUBT

hristian's will to continue on his quest lessened with every laborious step that he took. He had walked for several miles with no food, no water, and no shade. He was in trouble and desperately needed to find some form of shelter. The merciless sun unleashed wave after wave of light and fiery heat, robbing Christian of his strength and blurring his eyesight. His fall into Dead Man's Swamp left him covered from the chest down in a combination of mud and sludge that smelled awful. The heat magnified this smell and baked the muddy compound until it was as hard as concrete, adding serious weight on Christian, making it hard for him to move. Christian was forced to breathe slow and controlled breaths from his mouth because the stink made him want to puke. *Maybe I should go on home like Pliable and stop all this King and Celestial City stuff! I don't even know if this place is real! Maybe I should go home. I'll never make it. What if everyone else is right and this is all just a waste of time?*

Christian quieted his mind, gathered his thoughts, and searched within to find some form of motivation. He needed to find something that would give him a small spark or boost of energy. *The King would never give you more than you could bear, Chris.*[1] *It is when you are weak that He is strong.*[2] *He will never leave or forsake you!*[3]

Promises from the King, written in the Book, tumbled through Christian's mind and gave him comfort. He was trying to do it all on his own power and needed the King's help. Christian collapsed to his knees and asked the King for renewed strength and relief. *All I need is a few hours in the shade, my King.*

Opening his burning bloodshot eyes slowly, Christian was amazed at how strong he now felt! He quickly ran his hands across his body. He was still covered in smelly mud and sludge. He still had his burden tied to his back. Somehow though, everything was now more bearable. He rose and turned to continue his journey. His eyesight was clearer now and he could see that he was just a short distance away from an enormous batch of trees. *You came through! Thanks, King!*

....

[1] 1 Corinthians 10:13, [2] 2 Corinthians 12:10, [3] Deuteronomy 31:8

10
WORLDLY WISE

Christian was very happy to be travelling in the shade. The trees, some as tall as skyscrapers, were the perfect shield against the sun's powerful sunlight and heat with their thick trunks and enormous leaves. Resting at the base of one of these natural skyscrapers, Christian let his eyes follow one of the tree trunks in front of him from the base upwards until it disappeared into the afternoon sky. *I bet that no one could climb one of these to the top.*

He stood slowly and looked all around, his stomach rumbling with hunger pangs. *I wonder if any of these trees have any fruit on them.* As Christian walked, he noticed that the weight of his burden had returned in full, but the weight of his muddy encasement was just starting to return. He had to find food and he had to find it quickly. Christian turned to look right, and then quickly looked left. His heart began to pound heavily in his ears as fear and doubt threatened to reenter his mind. Closing his eyes, he began to inhale through his nose deeply, stopping abruptly by the return of the foul stench that came from his muddy prison. *Eeeeww!* Not allowing himself to panic, he switched to inhaling through his mouth. *Calm down! Only with a clear mind can you see.*

He followed the path as it turned left and curved around a group of towering trees. Just as the path began to take him back to the right, Christian noticed that two of the trees were spaced further apart than the others. He looked between them to find a smaller tree. *Yes!* Christian raised his arms triumphantly. Attached to its branches were the biggest, reddest, and sweetest-smelling apples he had ever seen! *All I have to do is get a few of those down and I'll be straight!*

Impulsively wrapping his arms around the trunk of the tree, Christian tried to lift himself, but the weight of all that he carried was too much for him to lift. He let go of the tree and searched nearby for a fallen branch or something that he could use to make a few apples fall from the tree. All he could find was a wooden staff just a few inches taller than he was, leaning against one of the trees. He looked to see if anyone was around; he saw no one so he picked up the staff. On it were beautiful markings carved all around. *Yep, this belongs to somebody. I'll just use it to knock down some of these apples and then put it back.*

Standing directly under the apple tree, Christian began to swing the staff carefully in order not to damage it, but it was too short. *Umm . . . Maybe I can just toss the staff.* Although it did strike a few, the hanging apples remained attached to the tree. He did this many more times with the same result before kicking the tree out of frustration. *Darn it!* His kick shook the entire tree with such force that more than enough of the apples fell to the ground. *Finally! I can eat!* He quickly bent down to claim one of his prizes and bit into its appetizing skin. *This is the best apple I ever tasted!*

"Bravo! Young man! Bravo!"

Christian turned swiftly to find a tall, slender man dressed in a white suit and a red tie walking toward him. A white brim with a red ribbon around it covered his shoulder-length hair. *That hair has to be permed.* No black guys Christian knew had natural hair that wavy. The man's gator-skinned shoes were spotless and colored to match the rest of his attire. *This guy reminds me of Mike in his Smooth Criminal video.*

As the man continued his approach, Christian changed his stance and raised the staff in a protective manner. The man stopped just beyond the reach of his swing. With his hands raised, he began to smile. Christian could see the bling of a gold cap covering one of his top teeth.

"Now there's no need for that, Lil' Man. I assure you that I am perfectly harmless. I just happened to be travelin' on this here road just in time to see you tryin' to get yourself some food." The man paused as if he expected Christian to respond. Christian not only remained silent, but also kept his stance, eyeing the man suspiciously.

"I knew it! Yessiree! I knew it the moment I saw you!" The man clapped his hands and placed a finger on his temple. "I said to myself, Worldly, this is a sharp young man. Yes sir, very sharp indeed! I have always admired those who could overcome a handicap and then use that handicap to elevate themselves to a better place." The man paused, closed one eye a little as to focus all his sight through the other eye, and then nodded as his gaze sized up Christian.

"I can see that you have the heart of a lion, the courage of a tiger, and the strength of a bull. How else could you have made it this far all wrapped up in that there earthly encasement?" He pointed to the dried mud and sludge covering Christian before continuing. "Not a lot of folk make it out of Dead Man's Swamp, hence the name you know." He chuckled to himself. "And then, to have the strength to travel all this way with the weight and that horrendous smell all over you . . . humph! You're a better man than me!"

Christian began to ease up a little. *Maybe he can help me. He seems to know this place very well.* Besides, he still had the staff and it felt solid enough to bust this guy's head wide open, if needed.

Seeing that Christian was softening, the man removed his hat, and bowing, he extended his right hand. "I am called Worldly Wise, primarily because I am smarter than most other guys. I am *the* jack of all trades, but the master of none. I don't claim to know everything, but about everything I know some!"

What a character! Christian thought as he totally relaxed and lowered the staff. While trying not to laugh, he raised his hand and introduced himself to this colorful cat.

"Christian. Now that's a strong name. No wonder you have such spirit and will. Strength of heart is a good thing, but strength of the mind is better still." He pointed to the staff before continuing, "You have the look of a man on a mission, now this is very true, but you lack the aptitude and wisdom, to safely follow thru. That staff in your hand is mine. To you it's a simple stick. But if you trust and give it to me, I'll make it do magic tricks!" He gestured for Christian to give him back the staff.

Christian was mesmerized by the man's smooth talk, but still felt reluctant to give up his only form of protection. However, he did say that he would return it to its owner. "How do I know that this is yours?"

"Well, I guess since there's no physical evidence that I can produce to show ownership of that staff, you will have to use discernment."

Christian, having no idea what that meant, replied, "Di-what-ment?"

"Di-surn-ment . . . discernment! It means to go with your gut. You know, follow your instincts! Now I can really help you, Lil' Man, but only if you allow me to."

Christian pondered his next move carefully and then decided to give Worldly Wise the staff. He felt it was the right thing to do. The instant the staff was in the hands of Worldly Wise, it was surrounded by a blue light—the same blue light that came from the video boxes in D'City. Worldly Wise slowly lowered the staff, tapped Christian's leg three times, and then said, "Watch my power, boy! Watch my shine! Watch what's going to happen from me tapping your leg three times! Now, appreciation will be due, after your celebration is thru and from me, an apology as well! Because as you can see, from your prison you are free, but I could do nothing about the smell! Voila!"

Instantly the mud and sludge simply became dust and fell to the ground. Christian was filled with so much joy that he began to do an old school dance called "The Running Man." The breeze felt especially refreshing as it blew past the parts of his body now freed because of Worldly Wise.

"Thank you, thank you, thank you, Mr. Wise!" Christian shouted as he began to shake the man's hand wildly. "Thank you so very much! Sorry that I didn't trust you at first. I'm from the city and well, we don't trust anybody we don't know!"

"No worries, Lil' Man. Heck, I would've been the same way had I been in your shoes. Now get ready to take a seat." With these words spoken, Worldly Wise began to twirl the glowing staff over his head. "That's right! We're about to take a load off our feet! Now that you are free, the next thing you will need is food of all kinds, your face you must feed!" And just like that, right out of thin air, appeared a table and chairs with enough food to feed an army! Christian could hardly believe his eyes.

The two sat, ate, and talked about all that had happened to Christian until now. During their conversation, Christian was amazed at the knowledge Worldly Wise possessed about the King, His Son, and the Book. *He really is a wise man! How lucky I am to have met this guy!* Christian thought as he stuffed the last bite of Dutch apple cheesecake in his mouth. How full he was! Patting his belly, he burped loudly and sighed.

This made Worldly Wise smile. "Are you full, Lil' Man?" Christian simply nodded in reply. He was too full to speak.

"Good! Good! Never let it be said that Worldly Wise does not know how to deliver a spread! You know, Christian, I like you. I think you are a cool kid. So I'm gonna let you in on a little secret." Worldly Wise covered his mouth with the back of his hand and leaned in very close to Christian before continuing. He was almost whispering as if someone might be listening. "I know of a secret shortcut that leads to the Shepherd's Gate. It reduces your travel time by more than half!"

"Really?!" Christian almost screamed. This excited him because the sooner he got to the Gate, the sooner he could get to the Cross, and the sooner he could get rid of this stupid burden.

"Sure, Lil' Man! Now I don't normally do this, but as soon as you are ready to go, I will take you to the entrance."

Christian instantly leaped from his seat surprised at his swiftness, considering the heaviness of his burden. "I'm ready now!" he said loudly.

"Okay! Well, let's get goin' then," said Worldly Wise, as he snapped his fingers to make everything disappear.

Worldly Wise led Christian back to the path, turned right, and continued to go forward for some time before stopping next to a large group of bushes. Smiling at Christian, Worldly Wise tapped his staff on the ground three times and the bushes parted to reveal a hidden path that led up a hill.

"There you go, Lil' Man! The shortcut to Shepherd's Gate just like I said! All you gotta do is follow this path up to the top of the hill, then back down the other side. You'll be at that ole' Gate before you know it!"

Christian turned to follow the path, then stopped. Something didn't seem right. He turned to face Worldly Wise. "Evangelist told me never to stray from the King's Path and well . . ." Christian turned to view the shortcut before continuing. "This seems to lead me away from it."

"Awwww. Come on now, Christian! This couldn't be a secret shortcut if it were in plain sight and followed the path directly! The path that leads to the King is narrow and straight. Correct?" He kneeled on the side of Christian. He placed his

left hand on Christian's shoulder and guided Christian's eyes with his right hand pointing the staff forward. "Everybody knows that the shortest distance between where you're at and where you wanna be is a straight line. Look, it doesn't get any straighter. Nor does the path get any narrower than this one. Evangelist gave you very good advice indeed, but I'm willing to bet that he doesn't even know about this here shortcut. Now it's totally up to you: you can go up and get to the Gate quicker this way or go with your gut and take the longer way around the hill."

Christian was never so confused in his life. Worldly Wise had been so nice to him not only freeing and feeding him, but helping him get to the Gate sooner. Christian wanted to sprint right up the hill and get this part of his journey over, but the warning from Evangelist played softly in his mind. He looked into the eyes of Worldly Wise, hoping to find an answer.

After a long pause, Christian gave his response. "Okay. You're probably right. Maybe Evangelist doesn't know about this shortcut." Christian turned quickly and gave Worldly Wise a hug. "Thank you for all your help, Worldly Wise."

The hug caught Worldly Wise offguard. It had been a long time since he had received any form of affection from someone. "Oh . . . um . . . well, it was nothing really. Just doing what I have to do." He looked around nervously. "Now off you go! I must close the entryway before everyone travelling along this road will know our little secret!"

Christian started to jog along this newfound path full of expected wonder, feeling the same way that all children feel when tucked into bed on Christmas Eve. He couldn't wait to get on the other side of the hill. Christian turned to wave one last time to the man who had helped him so much, but noticed he was no longer there. The entrance had been sealed. *Thanks again, Worldly*, Christian thought as continued up the hill.

Worldly Wise stood staring at the group of bushes that hid the secret shortcut. "Seemed like a pretty cool kid," he muttered as he left to ensnare another gullible fool.

11

BAMBOOZLED!

Christian moved up the hill quickly and with very little effort, amazed at how his climb was more like riding an escalator. He wondered if it was the ease of the path, the rest combined with the food, or the absence of all the mud that made him stronger, but he decided to take a break. If the rest of the climb was this easy, he should reach the top in no time at all. He sat and pulled one of the apples he had gathered from the pocket of his jeans. He was just about to take a bite when he noticed little white maggots crawling all over the apple. "Agghhh!" He screamed as he threw the apple and shook his hands to make sure that there were no maggots on them. The beautiful red skin had turned brown and ugly.

Quickly pulling the other apples from his denim pockets, he discovered that they too were now rotten. Christian threw the apples far away from him and then turned his pockets inside out. He wildly swept away a few remaining maggots from his pockets and attempted to stomp them quickly. He began to panic. It was like he could feel the little worm-like insects crawling all over his skin. *How could the apples be rotten already? I just picked them up a few hours ago. Man, that's crazy!*

Christian pulled himself together and began to follow the path up the hill. It was still a very simple climb, but it looked very different. Rock formations hanging over the path gave

Christian the creeps. They were all shaped like giant creatures with deformed faces, their bodies arched over the path as if waiting to attack. He continued to move slowly and carefully, his heart was beating very hard and fast. The air became thin and the sky became dark as he considered turning back. No! He had to keep going. Wide-eyed and focused, Christian kept his gaze upwards on the head and shoulders of the distorted creatures. He would have to be ready if one of these came to life and attacked him.

Suddenly, his burden became an almost unbearable weight on his back. The weight change was so extreme and so fast that Christian was forced to the ground on his hands and knees. He now knew that he had made a wrong choice. Worldly Wise had misled him. Sweat poured down his face as he began to crawl his way upwards. *I gotta get out of this trap.* His determination was now fueled by his anger toward Worldly Wise. Each crawling movement Christian made became harder than the last as his burden continued to get heavier.

CAPLOOOOOM!

The sound of thunder angrily rolling across the invisible sky stopped Christian dead in his tracks.

CAPLOOOOOOOOM! CAPLOO . . . CAPLOO . . . CA-PLOOOOOOM!

The thunderous sounds shook the very ground that he was forced to crawl on.

CAPLOOOOOOOOM!

Christian sat up and covered his ears.

CAPLOOOOOOM!

The vibrations from the explosive sounds combined with fear caused his teeth to chatter.

CAPLOOOOOOOOOOM!

"NOOOOOOOOOO . . . Stop it!" Christian screamed in desperation.

As soon as he yelled stop, the thunderous booms ceased. Christian slowly removed his hands from his ears. *What? The sounds have stopped!* Did he have that kind of power? He turned his attention upwards and could see that the top of the hill was just a short distance from where he was. *I can do this.*

Christian had to draw on all of his strength to get up to the top of the hill as his burden began to press down upon him with every second that passed. Covering the very short distance to the top seemed to take an eternity.

Once at the top, Christian was amazed at how quiet it was. There was no sound of the wind, no chirping of birds, there was nothing, except the sound of his own heavy breathing. The silence itself had an oppressive weight, causing Christian to feel uneasy. All of a sudden . . .

"You are doomed! Doomed I say! You will never make it off this mountain!" The sound of several voices screamed in unison. Men, women, and beasts all yelled together in one echoing voice, "Who are you to leave the good life that the Wicked Prince has given you? You belong to him!"

Christian was more frightened than he had ever been in his entire life. He looked around frantically, but he could see no one in the darkness. He fell to his knees, hugged himself, and began to cry. "Why won't you just leave me alone?" Christian screamed in despair.

The ground beneath him began to shake and rumble with the effects of an earthquake. The legion of voices now became one horrifying voice that chilled Christian to the bone. "Because you are mine, boy! You belong to me mind, body, and soul!" the deep voice proclaimed.

Christian knew this had to be the voice of the Wicked Prince, and his heart was struck with a paralyzing fear. He placed his head to the ground and said the only thing he could now think of. "King, help me! Please!"

"What are you doing up here?" This voice was familiar though the tone was hard and stern. "Christian! Get up and tell me why you are up here!" commanded the voice.

Christian looked up slowly, with eyes full of tears, to see Evangelist standing over him, his arms folded in front of his chest. His face held a look of father-like anger. Christian suddenly felt ashamed and embarrassed to be in his current predicament. He didn't know where to begin his explanation or if he even wanted to try. "I'm sorry, Evangelist," Christian forced through his sobs. "I was tired and hungry. I know you told me not to stray from the path, but Worldly . . ."

"What??!" Evangelist quickly interrupted sounding angrier than before. "You listened to that slithery snake? That misled fool who believes that he alone knows the secrets of the universe? Christian, how could you fall for that swindler's scheme?"

Christian shouted while sobbing so hard that he could barely speak. "I told you! I was tired and hungry! He was nice to me! He fed me and took away some of my burden! He told me that this shortcut would lead me to the Shepherd's Gate in half the time! Why shouldn't I believe him? Where were you when I needed help?"

Evangelist changed his look of anger to a look of compassion and pity. "I'm sorry, Chris, but I told you to stay on the King's Path no matter what. Worldly Wise can be very persuasive if you fall for his charismatic charm. He has ensnared many others. You need to be on guard and stay focused."

"I know. I'm sorry. I wanted the easier path. It was my fault." Christian's voice was now soft and full of fatigue. He was very glad that Evangelist was here, but Christian was sad to have disappointed him so much.

He was surprised at how small and narrow the entrance was.

"Look, Chris. Worldly was once the most intelligent man in all the land and many people would travel from all over to hear his wise interpretations of the world's most complicated problems. He was so sought after that he believed himself smarter than the King. He began to use his logic to challenge all the King had written in the Book. And even though he knows the Book cover to cover, his lack of faith has blinded him to the Book's truths. Don't beat yourself up too much, Chris, for Worldly Wise has bamboozled and tricked many along this road which is why, from time to time, I travel up this hill by order of the King to try and save as many as I can from this trap of his."

"You mean Worldly Wise doesn't know that the King knows about his secret path?" Christian asked.

"Not a clue." Evangelist gave Christian a wink and a smile before continuing. "There is nothing that the King doesn't know about or sees. He is always watching out for those who choose to find Him. Now let's get you back on the right track!" And with that, Evangelist lovingly guided Christian down the hill, back to the path that led to the Shepherd's Gate.

12

THE SHEPHERD'S GATE

*T*hat light is almost brighter than the sun itself, Christian thought, as he shielded his eyes from the brilliance radiating from a lamp above the Gate. He quickened his steps with all the energy he could muster. *I made it!* Upon reaching his destination, he was surprised at its plainness and how small and narrow the entrance was; it was nothing like the ornate grand structure he imagined it to be. Standing on the threshold, Christian read the sign above the door that was written in large unmistakable letters, "Knock and it will be opened to you."[1] Anxiously, he reached out his hand and boldly knocked on the heavy paneled door, noticing a small door-like opening, no bigger than a man's fist, built in the middle about eye-level. *Hmmm . . . That's strange, but oh, I have to get in!* Christian anxiously thought, as he raised his fist to knock again.

"Who's there?" A voice called out as the tiny door flew open suddenly. Intense brown eyes surrounded by wrinkles peered out at Christian. Christian stepped backwards with surprise.

"Uh. My name is Christian."

"Did you come from the City of Destruction?" The voice was deep, yet kind, reminding Christian of Gramps' voice. The similarity gave him courage to continue.

"Yes, and I really want to see the King at the Celestial City."

"How did you come to know of this Gate?"

"I met Evangelist and he told me."

As soon as the words left Christian's mouth, the large heavy paneled door of the Gate swung open quickly. Swoosh . . . Thud!

Christian felt the air move beside his ear as something whizzed past. The Gatekeeper grabbed his arm yanking him hard inside before slamming the door and securing both latches.

Thud . . . Thud.

Startled, his arm stinging from the Gatekeeper's viselike grip, Christian asked, "Why did you do that?"

"Let me introduce myself," said the grey-haired bearded man in a calm voice. "My name is Goodwill and you are very safe here now. Now you belong to the King—you are His. But, just on the other side of the hill, there is a castle belonging to the Wicked Prince. He and his minions will stop at nothing to keep those belonging to him from entering the King's Way. They would rather shoot them dead with arrows than see them give their allegiance to the King." Christian shuddered to think what would have happened if he was pulled through the door a second too late.

Goodwill continued, "The King has given me the important task of carefully watching at the Shepherd's Gate and letting anyone enter who desires to go to Him. He protects all who seek to follow Him."

"Why is it called the Shepherd's Gate?" Christian asked, looking around not seeing anything that resembled a shepherd or sheep anywhere.

Goodwill smiled a big warm smile, his thoughts taking him somewhere else for a fleeting moment. "It belongs to the Good Shepherd." He placed a hand gently on Christian's shoulder. "This Gate was built by Him and is the only way to the King. The Good Shepherd loves everyone and desires them all to come to the King. That's why He has directed me to let all who knock enter. No one, no matter how big their burden or where they came from, will ever be turned away or ignored." Goodwill smiled that warmhearted smile again, his eyes revealing that his thoughts went to that far-off place again. "You'll meet the Good Shepherd soon enough, Christian. Everyone who meets Him never forgets Him. Never."

Something about the way that Goodwill talked about the Good Shepherd made Christian feel loved and treasured. He couldn't wait to meet this Good Shepherd! He tried to imagine what He would look like, but Goodwill's question jarred him back to the present.

"Why are you travelling alone in your quest of the Celestial City, Christian? Where is your family?"

Christian looked down at the gravel path at his feet and cleared his throat. "Well, my mom and little sister are still living in the City of Destruction. They didn't want to leave. My grandfather, Gramps, is already in the Celestial City." Christian stopped talking, as that gloomy day passed through his mind like dark storm clouds threatening to spill tears.

Goodwill seemed to sense Christian's sadness, and putting his hand reassuringly on his shoulder, quietly spoke. "Since your Gramps is with the King, he would have passed through this very Gate, you know. Of course, you will not see him again until you reach the Celestial City, but you can be assured that he is cheering you on in your journey."

Christian looked up into Goodwill's kind, honest eyes, his own eyes widening in excitement. "For real? Do you really think so?"

Goodwill smiled. "Yes. Now, it's getting late. Why don't we get you some food and you can rest at my place tonight and be on your way in the morning?"

The next morning, Christian awoke to a mouth-watering aroma and his stomach rumbled. He sat up in bed, but immediately forgetting about the heavy burden, quickly tumbled out of bed onto the floor. Rubbing his sore shoulder and mumbling about that nuisance, he stood up slowly. Upon reaching the dining room, Christian was warmly greeted by Goodwill.

"Good morning, Christian. Come eat an all-you-can-eat breakfast just for you, provided by the Good Shepherd Himself." Goodwill smiled that kind smile again as he watched Christian eat forkful after forkful of scrambled eggs, pancakes with warm maple syrup, grits, bacon, washing it down with the freshest orange juice he ever tasted. "The Good Shepherd takes very good care of us, doesn't He?"

Christian nodded as he wiped his mouth. He was stuffed! "So, where does the King's Path go next?"

"Well, down the path a little ways is the House of the Interpreter. You can't miss his place. If you choose to stop there, I'm quite sure he will show you great and wonderful stories and pictures from the King Himself if you ask."

Christian couldn't wait to continue on his journey! He stood up and shifted the burden in an attempt to even the weight on his back.

"The Place of the Cross is not too far now, Christian." Goodwill replied, noticing Christian's awkward movement. "It is the place where your burden will fall off your back, never to be seen or worn again. Not by anything you have done or could do, Christian. It is a free gift from the One who loves you and gave His life so you can be with the King." He walked Christian to the door and pointed to the gravel path. "See this straight and narrow path? That is the path you must take. The King's Path is always straight and narrow. You may come across other paths that look easier, but don't be fooled. Always look for and travel on the straight and narrow path." And with that, Goodwill patted Christian on the back. "Go now, Christian. Focus on the King and safe travels!"

....

[1] Matthew 7:7 NIV

13
THE INTERPRETER

efreshed and well-rested from his stay with Goodwill, Christian couldn't remember the last time when he felt so good. The mixture of the sun's warm, gentle rays, the cheerful sounds of chatting birds, and the cool fresh air invigorated him as he whistled along. Soon, he spotted a large two-story brick house off the side of the path, surrounded by a grove of mature oak trees. *That must be the House of the Interpreter. Goodwill said that I couldn't miss it.*

Following the gravel path to the front door, Christian noticed a brass door knocker shaped in the form of a lion's head. *That's cool.* He shifted the Book into his left hand and with his right hand lifted the round brass ring that was securely fastened in the lion's mouth. Knock. Knock. Knock. Christian could hear the soft shuffle of feet and the click of the lock. The door opened slightly and a raspy voice called out.

"Who's there?"

"I am Christian and I'm on my way to see the King. Goodwill told me I could stop here."

The door opened wider, revealing a short, ancient-looking bearded man, smiling broadly. "Come in, come in! Goodwill is my friend! And any King's kid is welcome here!" He motioned Christian inside with a wide sweep of his arm. "Come, come! Come in and make yourself at home!"

Christian stepped over the threshold and found himself in a small entryway illuminated only by a dim bronze chandelier suspended from the ceiling. The Interpreter closed the door and turned to Christian, extending his hand. "I'm the Interpreter and it's a pleasure to meet you. Christian did you say your name was?"

Christian nodded and couldn't help but stare at this man. He looked like someone straight out of a storybook with his immaculate white pantsuit that hung on his thin frame and small wire-rimmed spectacles that balanced on his protruding nose. The elderly man didn't seem to notice his stares and motioned Christian to follow him. Together, they walked down a short dark paneled hallway, Christian being careful not to step on the heels of the stooped-over Interpreter who walked in small steps, leaning heavily on an intricately carved wooden cane.

The Interpreter led Christian to a comfortable sitting room with shelves overloaded with books, lining all four walls. "Sit down, Christian, and make yourself at home." Christian didn't think twice, plopping himself down on the plush oversized sofa, as the Interpreter slowly lowered himself in a nearby armchair, leaning on his cane for support.

Glancing around the room, Christian was intrigued with the various assortments of mismatched items he noticed on various shelves. A slingshot. A sash colored in the hues of a rainbow. *Must be from a robe of some kind.* A statue in the form of a bronze snake on a pole. A jar with crumbs of some kind inside. A crown worthy to be worn on a queen's head. A miniature replica of a ship with sails. A cross with a crown of thorns next to it. *Cool. I have to ask the Interpreter about these.*

"So, Christian, tell me of your journey thus far." And so Christian began to excitedly retell his adventures while the Interpreter listened intently to every word.

After spending most of the morning reliving his adventures about Gramps, Evangelist, Obstinate and Pliable, the Dead Man's Swamp, Worldly Wise, and the Shepherd's Gate, Christian suddenly remembered Goodwill's suggestion. "Goodwill told me that you have many stories and pictures from the King. Would you show them to me?" He paused. "Please?"

The Interpreter shifted in his chair and tapped his cane on the floor. "I'd be happy to," he replied, "when you are ready."

"Oh, I'm ready now!" If it wasn't for the burden, Christian would have leaped up from the couch.

The Interpreter smiled at Christian's enthusiasm. "Let's eat something first and then I will show you." He reached over and rang a little silver bell. Minutes later, a cheerful stout woman appeared carrying a tray of ham and cheese sandwiches, chips and fruit, of which the Interpreter and Christian enjoyed every bite.

Swallowing the last bite of his sandwich, Christian stood up. "Can we go now?"

The Interpreter nodded, and then paused for a long moment, stroking his long white beard. "Actually, Christian, I think I should first show you the stained glass window." He stood up and hobbled determinedly down the long, dark, paneled hallway with Christian following close behind, noticing the numerous closed doors on each side. Christian wondered what mysteries lay behind them. Finally, the Interpreter stopped in front of the last door in the corridor and paused, bowing his head.

Opening the door slowly, almost reverently, the Interpreter gestured for Christian to enter first. Upon entering the room, Christian gasped in pure awe. Never before had he ever seen something so beautiful, and yet so captivating. He couldn't take his eyes off of the artistic masterpiece. The bright afternoon sun radiated through a large stained glass window reaching from floor to ceiling, illuminating the room in every hue imaginable. While the colors impressed Christian, it was the Man Himself that left him speechless.

The Man, his body filling most of the height and width of the window, wore a simple white robe draped by a cobalt blue sash. A halo of bright yellow encircled His head, and in His left hand, He held a wooden staff, shaped like a candy cane. His strong right arm tightly held a little lamb.

Chris fell to his knees, his heart bursting with love for the Good Shepherd.

Thoughts and questions flooded Christian's mind and came in rapid succession, like the darts fired from his Nerf gun. Sensing the war zone of wonderment going on inside Christian, the Interpreter laid a timeworn hand on Christian's shoulder. "This is the Good Shepherd, Christian," he whispered.

Christian nodded. He had sensed the answer deep within his being long before the Interpreter spoke it.

After a moment's pause, the Interpreter answered. "The Good Shepherd is the King's Son, Christian. His kids are like that lamb. Just like a shepherd takes great care of his sheep, so the Good Shepherd takes great care of all belonging to Him. He knows His kids and calls them by name. If they get lost, He goes to look for them and carries them to safety. Nothing can take away the Good Shepherd's love for His lambs. Nothing." Christian pointed to the words etched in gold at the bottom of the window and read them aloud. "He gathers the lambs in his arms and carries them close to his heart."[1]

"So . . ." He paused. "I'm that lamb." Christian looked up at the Interpreter. The Interpreter nodded slowly, his eyes moistening with joy that Christian had met the Good Shepherd. Instinctively, Christian fell to his knees with arms outstretched in reverence, his heart bursting with love and thanks to the Good Shepherd for loving him that much! *I will never forget the Good Shepherd. Never ever.*

After a long moment of silence, Christian looked up at the Interpreter, with eyes wide. "Thanks for showing me this! Can I see and hear the other stories now that Goodwill told me about?"

Helping Christian to his feet because of the burden's weight, the Interpreter chuckled. "Come. This house is full of many wonderful stories from the King." Together, they spent the rest of the afternoon and into the evening enjoying the stories from the King about His Son and the other pilgrims that went before them: Abraham, Joseph, Moses, Daniel, David, Esther, Mary, Paul, to name a few. Christian was surprised to learn that the captivating objects he noticed earlier on the bookshelves once belonged to these pilgrims.

That night, Christian fell fast asleep, his head full of wonderful dreams and his heart full of thanks to the King for all he saw and heard.

....

[1] Isaiah 40:11 NIV

14

FREE AT LAST!

Christian awoke with a jolt. The bright morning sun was already streaming through the windows, waking him from his peaceful sleep. He had been sleeping so soundly, he almost forgot what day it was. *How could I forget?* This was the day that he anticipated since that day not so long ago. That day when he first noticed the sack was on his back.

Getting up from the comfortable oversized bed, Christian shivered with excitement. *Today I lay my burden down.* He rushed out of the room to meet the Interpreter, finding him sitting at the dining room table with a delicious meal of waffles with strawberries, sausage, and grits set on the table. "Good morning, Christian. Looks like you slept well last night." Christian nodded and bowed his head for a quick prayer of thanks. He began to eat.

"Whoa. Slow down, Christian, and chew your food. No use rushing."

In between mouthfuls of grits and waffle, Christian replied, "Yeah, I know. It's just I can't wait to get this burden off my back. If you had to carry what I have to carry, you'd understand."

The Interpreter smiled. "All of us had some burden to bear. Some were even larger than yours before we came to the Place of the Cross. If it weren't for the trees surrounding the

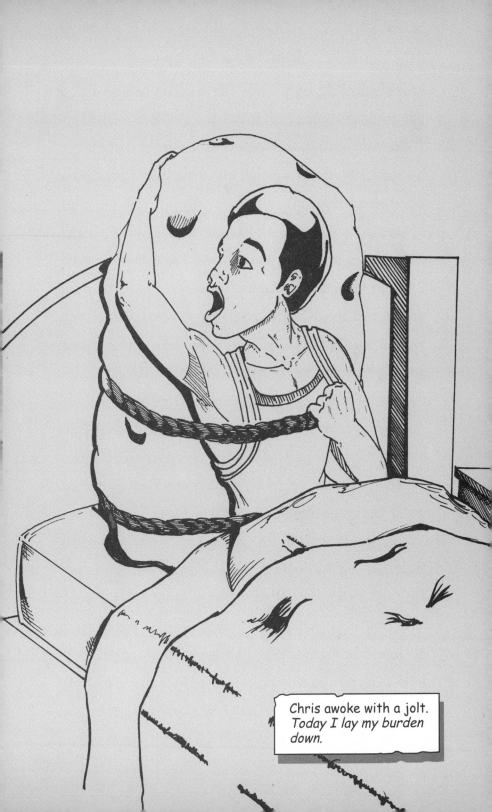

Chris awoke with a jolt.
*Today I lay my burden
down.*

house, you could see it. It won't be long now before you lose that burden for good."

Christian nodded and finished the last bit of waffle left on his plate. He wiped his mouth with the back of his hand and stood up quickly. "I'm ready now."

Standing at the door, the Interpreter gave Christian heartfelt parting words. "I've enjoyed your company very much, Christian. Remember what you've seen and heard here and don't forget about your Good Shepherd who loves you very much. He will always watch over you." Full of thanks but eager to get going to be rid of the weight on his back, Christian hugged the Interpreter and trotted down the path.

Christian couldn't contain his excitement. He was so close to the place where he would lose his burden forever! He continued to walk fast, not caring about his back aching tremendously under the weight. *Shouldn't be too far now.*

Then he saw it off on the right side of the path and stared. It was nothing like he thought it would be. *This is the place? For real? It's so plain. Nothin' special about it. Who would even notice it?* Christian almost stopped in awe and disbelief, but remembering the cross's promise, excitedly he ran. Away from all his past wrong choices. Away from shame and guilt and regret. With every ounce of energy and strength he had, Christian ran toward the two crossed wooden beams, tears streaming down his cheeks. He ran toward the King's love. Toward freedom. Toward eternal life.

Arriving at the foot of the cross, Christian collapsed to his knees. He was mentally and physically exhausted. He was tired of his doubts and tired of carrying the shame and guilt of wrong choices and tired of trying to make right choices on his own strength.

Looking up at the simple structure in front of him, Christian remembered the story of the King's Son that the Interpreter told him. He recalled every vivid detail of when the King's Son visited D'City. Although He was kind to everyone and taught them about the King, the people of D'City hated Him and were very mean to Him. They brutally nailed Him to a wooden cross, the worst punishment for a criminal, although He did nothing wrong. Christian cried at the unfairness of it all. *The King's Son did nothing wrong, and yet He died the horrible death of a murderer.*

"However," the Interpreter had said, "it was the King's plan all along that His Son would die, since all those carrying a burden could never live with Him in the Celestial City. By dying," the Interpreter explained, "the King's Son took everyone's burdens on Himself. The good news is that the King's Son didn't stay dead, but rose with power three days later, defeating death once and for all. Because of what the King's Son did so lovingly and sacrificially, now everyone who believes in Him will be able to live with the King forever in the Celestial City."

Christian's tears turned to heavy sobs. "I'm so sorry, King, for making wrong choices. I need Your help. I do believe Your promises. I know that it's true that Your Son died in my place to take away my burden. Please help me. I want to follow You." Suddenly, Christian felt warm all over as a soft yellow light surrounded his entire body.

Snap! Snap! Snap!

The once indestructible ropes that held his burden in place were now removed with ease by what appeared to be three glowing beings with wings standing in front of him. Christian blinked in amazement and felt the burden roll off his back— gone. He looked around and couldn't see it anywhere.

"Peace to you!" One of the Beings spoke. "We are the Shining Ones sent by the King and are here to give you gifts. Free gifts given to you by the King because of His never-ending love for you."

The first Shining One continued, "On behalf of the King and His Son, I give you the gift of having your burden gone forever. The King's Son has rescued you from the captivity of carrying it. All of your wrong choices in the past, present, and future are forgiven and forgotten. Every single one of them."

The once-indestructible ropes were removed with ease by three glowing beings.

Forever. Christian wrapped his arms around the base of the thick wooden cross and wept at the thought. He was so thankful to the King's Son. *He has really taken away my burden forever.*

The second Shining One spoke next. "The King has sent Me to give you a brand-new set of clothes. Your new clothes will show others that you are different. You are a King's kid now and are part of the King's family." Christian looked down, his eyes wide. His mud-stained smelly clothes were transformed into a brand-new shining white T-shirt and durable khaki cargo pants. *Wow! Pants with cool pockets! Bet the Book can fit into one of them!* Sure enough, it did.

"And now you have a place that is being prepared for you in the Celestial City." The third Shining One broke His silence. "Here is a Scroll for you. You need to read it. It will guide you into all truth. Keep it with you at all times. You will be asked for it when you arrive at the majestic gates of the Celestial City." Christian received the ivory scroll in a container with a strap attached. On the strap, he noticed unfamiliar markings, looking nothing at all like English letters. The Shining One noticed his bewilderment. "That is Hebrew. The ancient language of the King." Christian traced the letters with his finger. "What does it say?"

"The key to life everlasting."

Securely fastening the scroll inside the holder and strapping it over his shoulder, Christian found himself leaping for joy. "Thank you! Thank you!"

The Shining Ones smiled, and holding up their right hands, they spoke a blessing over Christian in unison. "The King bless you and keep you; the King make His face shine upon you and be gracious to you; the King turn His face toward you and give you peace."[1] And with that, the Shining Ones vanished as quickly as they came.

Christian stood there, stunned. *I will never forget this. Thanks, King and Your Son, for everything!*

Whistling, he turned and headed back to the King's Path. Feeling free at last, he began to jog down the path.

....

[1] Numbers 6:24–26 NIV

15

HILL OF DIFFICULTY

Christian couldn't believe how good he was feeling as he childishly skipped down the King's Path! It had been such a long time since he felt lighthearted and free. He had new clothes, new focus, and most of all, a new sense of hope. *I've got nothin' to worry about! Look at me now! Whuuut! DOODA! DOOMP! DOOMP! I'm a King's kid!* Christian sang this verse in his mind repeatedly as he danced the Dougie down the path that led to eternal peace and harmony.

His celebration of song and dance came to an immediate stop as he noticed that the road on which he was travelling had suddenly come to an end. "Aw, MAAAAN!" He shouted before releasing a heavy sigh. *I spoke too soon!* Christian thought, shaking his head.

The road did come to end, but there was no question where the path led. The King's way was mapped out by the many footprints left by those who once stood where he now stood—footprints that led his gaze up the side of an enormous hill that loomed menacingly in front of him proving there was no other way to get around it.

Oh well. Ain't nothin' to it, but to do it, Christian thought as he started to jog up the hillside. The hillside was covered with rough stones and very sharp rocks that dug into the soles of his shoes. The sharp rocks were solid parts of the hill, but the stones were loose cover like the sand on a beach, so Christian moved carefully out of fear of sliding back down to the bottom of the hill. The hillside had become so steep that it was impossible to climb without using his hands as well as his feet.

MAAAN! This is insane, he thought. *There's no way I could have made this climb yesterday with that burden tied to my back!* Christian continued to climb for quite a while before the steepness of the hillside changed in a way that allowed him to walk again. He was very happy to be standing and not bear-crawling his way up the hill. His hands, covered in dirt, were sore and bleeding.

Just as he was trying to muster up a little more strength to continue, Christian came to a beautiful wooden gazebo, painted white, near the path. Walking toward it, Christian found comfortable seats lined with sky blue pillows. Standing in the center, to Christian's delight, was a table with a tall, clear pitcher filled to the rim with red Kool-Aid and freshly cut lemons.

Christian poured himself a cup and drank it swiftly. "Ah yes! Sweet and sour, just like my mama makes it!" Pouring another cup, Christian removed the cylinder that held the scroll from around his shoulders and sat down. He noticed an unmistakable plaque that read: "Built for all weary pilgrims that follow Me. May you have peace and rest." This place had to be built by order of the King! Who else would have known how to make his favorite Kool-Aid and have it waiting for his arrival?

There's no way I could have made this climb yesterday with that burden! Chris thought.

Cool jasmine-scented air filled the gazebo, energizing and relaxing Christian at the same time. After he awoke from a short nap, he found the sun starting to set, blanketing the sky with yellow, orange, and crimson. He poured himself one more cup of the delicious Kool-Aid, hung the cylinder back over his shoulders, and hurried to complete his climb up the hill while he still had some daylight left.

Before reaching the top of the hill, Christian met two other boys sprinting in his direction. Their eyes were wide and filled with fright. As they spotted him, they began waving their arms wildly and screamed, "Go back! Stop! You gotta go back!"

Once the two young men reached Christian, the eldest boy grabbed him by his shoulders and blocked his path.

"Stop! Dude, you can't go that way! You're gonna . . . you're gonna . . . !" The boy released Christian and bent over gasping deeply for air.

"What's wrong with you guys? You're runnin' like you stole somethin'! You do know that you're runnin' in the wrong direction, right?"

The eldest boy was the first to catch his breath. Christian could see that something really had this one spooked. The boy worked hard to gather his composure, but failed to hide the fear that filled his eyes.

"My name's Timorous," he said before pointing to the other guy who seemed to be watching Christian closely, "and this is Mistrust." *That explains why this guy is so scared and the other dude is eyeballing me. Their names fit them,* Christian thought, while trying not to laugh.

"We were trying to make it to the Celestial City, you know. After climbing up this terrible hill, we found that the further we went, the more dangerous the road became, you know, so we decided to drop our mission and return home. You know?!"

"Yeah, Bro! We were walking along and whoa!" said Mistrust. "There were these two huge lions just chillin' on the road, waiting to have us for lunch...you know! We would have tried to sneak past them, but we couldn't tell whether or not they were asleep. I wasn't messin' with my hide, Homes, so we jetted."

Lions? Christian fought to control the fear now filling his own being. "Man! Now what am I gonna do?" He voiced his fear out loud to the two young men who definitely had to come from the Latin side of D'City.

"You need to come back with us," said Timorous. "You won't make it past those lions, Homes, for real!"

"I gotta try. Know what I'm sayin'? I've come too far from where I started from!" replied Christian. "If I go back now, I'll never get a chance to see the King."

"Well, if you keep going and the lions have you for dinner," said Mistrust, "meaning that they eat your little butt alive, you still won't get to see the King now, will you?"

"You got a point there, no doubt!" Christian paused and remembered all that Evangelist, Goodwill, and the wise Interpreter had told him. They told him that although he might often be afraid or in trouble, the King would surely watch over him, protect him, and take care of him. Always.

"Thanks for the warnin', but I can't go back," Christian answered courageously. "I gotta keep going. The King's got our back! Those lions—they can't touch us. We can do this, especially if we go together."

"You're either super brave or seriously crazy, Bro," said Timorous, now shaking his head in disbelief. "Either way, it's your funeral. We're out."

"It's cool. I understand. May the King watch over and protect you," said Christian, wishing he could persuade them to continue on this journey with him. He stood watching as they left to return to the City of Destruction, a place of hopelessness and isolation. Suddenly, he couldn't help but feel hopelessly alone as he continued to climb toward what might be a certain and painful end.

Please, King. Be with me.

16

THE PALACE BEAUTIFUL

The bright and harsh light of the sun was now replaced by the soft and subtle glow of the moon, just as Christian reached the top of the Hill of Difficulty. *Man I'm tired, hungry, and I can barely see now that the sun has gone down. I hope that I don't have to walk far to reach this palace,* Christian thought as he proceeded slowly, straining his eyes to see what was ahead of him. No matter how much he wanted to reach the palace quickly, he was in no hurry to reach the two savage lions that Timorous and Mistrust had told him about.

What am I gonna do? My new gear is so white and clean that I almost glow in the dark! There's no way I'm gonna be able to sneak past them. Anyway, I think that lions can smell a person coming a mile away. Christian released a sigh of hopelessness. *They're gonna be picking their teeth with my bones before I even know I'm dead!* Christian thought as the King's Path led him around a slight bend.

RHOOOARRRR! RHOOOARRR!

"AAGGHH!" Christian yelled as the sound of the lion's loud roars stopped him dead in his tracks. He was so deep in thought about how to get past the lions that he didn't notice how close he had come to them. He fell to his knees in order to keep himself from wetting his pants and covered his ears. "Oh King! What am I going to do? These terrible beasts will eat me for sure!" Christian screamed aloud, too horrified to even cry.

"What in tarnation!?" exclaimed Watchful, the gatekeeper, as he reached for his napkin. The unexpected roaring of the lions caused him to spill hot tea all over his shirt. "You two better be roaring at somethin' this time or I swear on the name of the King. Oops! Not supposed to swear!" Watchful covered his mouth in embarrassment. "I'm gonna turn you two into stuffed animals! I mean it this time!" Watchful yelled as he wiped off his shirt and headed for the front door. He had recently checked, as he often did, for any pilgrims who might be approaching the palace before pouring himself a cup of tea. The lions, being both cunning and observant, knew his routine and would sometimes roar just to disturb him, or so he believed.

"I'm serious this time! If you two don't stop all that racket, I'm gonna . . . oh my!" Watchful's eyes widened.

"Hey! Hey you, little pilgrim! Don't be frightened! The lions are both chained to very short leashes! Stay in the middle of the path and you shall not be harmed!" Watchful shouted in vain. The roars of the lions were too loud for his old voice to overcome. "Dagnabit! I'm getting too old for this!" Watchful placed two fingers in his mouth and released the loudest whistle that he could muster.

FHEEEERRRRRHHIT!

The mighty lions were instantly silenced by what Christian thought was a whistle. He picked himself up off the ground and tried to calm down. He was shaking so bad with fright that everything in his line of sight seemed to vibrate.

"Hello!" Watchful yelled at the frightened boy in order to get his attention. "There's no need to be afraid. The lions are both chained and cannot harm you as long as you stay directly in the middle of the path!"

Christian heard the man standing in the doorway waving his arms for him to come forward. *That old man is crazy! How do you know if you are directly in the middle of the path! It's so narrow here, a little to the left or the right and that's my hide for sure!* Christian looked at the lions (which had to be the largest lions he had ever seen) in order to gauge how far apart they were. Once he was comfortable with his visual measurement, he reluctantly moved forward putting one foot in front of the other, trembling uncontrollably.

The fierce beasts roared and growled, turning their beautifully maned heads in Christian's direction as he passed between them. They followed him with their eyes, but did not move otherwise. They continued to lay still and neither one even raised a paw to attack him! Breathing a sigh of relief, Christian pumped his fists in joy and started to run toward the man standing at the gate.

"I will fight with the King's help and power!"

"Well hello, little pilgrim. Come along, come along!" The doorkeeper said as he opened the gates to allow Christian to enter the palace grounds. "My name is Watchful and this is the Palace Beautiful."

"Wow!" Christian exclaimed as he followed Watchful through the elaborate garden that led to the palace. Never in his life had he seen a building like this one. Not even the mansions owned by D'City's wealthiest celebrities that appeared on that show, *Hot Cribs*, could compare to this.

"Who owns this place?" asked Christian as they stopped in front of two large white wooden doors with blue glass panes and golden hardware.

"Why, the King, of course. He built this palace for all pilgrims that travel to the Celestial City. Is that where you are headed?"

"Yep, that's where I'm going. Last night I stayed at the Interpreter's house and now I hope I get to rest here for the night." Christian's voice was full of hopeful excitement.

"Of course you can, Pilgrim. Anyone belonging to the King is a welcomed guest at the Palace Beautiful!" Watchful opened the doors to the most lavish and glorious foyer Christian had ever seen.

"Wait here, uh . . ." Watchful paused with expectation, not knowing the pilgrim's name.

"Oh, my bad! My name is Christian."

"Okay, Christian. The master of the house, Truth, is away fetching materials to help him with his special work. Wait here as I call on the lady of the house. She will see to any and all of your needs for the night."

"Got it. I'll wait right here."

Christian watched as the slender, scruffy old doorkeeper climbed the winding staircase with the ease of a teenager before disappearing down a corridor. While waiting, Christian entertained himself by taking in the sights of this impressive and massive foyer. The floors, stairs, trim, crown molding, and columns were all made of marble, the color of pearls, accented by dark cherry wood on the walls and stair railings. Christian was especially captivated by the design in the center of the grand foyer's floor. Inside two golden rings and a circle of maroon granite, a pearly white dove holding an olive branch made of green marble in its beak was in flight. It wasn't just the detailed expert craftsmanship that held his gaze; it looked like the dove was actually flapping its wings! Christian blinked hard and watched in amazement as the scenery within the ring of maroon granite changed as the dove soared through the circular sky toward a city behind large white walls.

"Now, I do believe that you are the cutest little thing to come up in here in quite a while!"

The soft and sweet voice startled Christian back to reality. He jumped. When he looked back at the marble floor, the dove was no longer moving. "I think you startled the boy, Mother," came a second soft voice with somewhat of an English accent.

"I think not, Hope. A boy who would travel this late must have a mighty brave heart indeed!" replied the first voice with a strong southern drawl.

Christian turned to view the owners of the sweet and delicate voices and stood frozen in place, his mouth agape. His eyes widened and he suddenly felt feverish. Before him stood a woman, two young ladies, and a little girl, each with sparkling eyes and a wide smile. He wanted to speak, but could not find words impressive enough to address such beautiful ladies.

"What's the matter, Sugar? Cat got your tongue?" The woman spoke. "My name is Discretion and these lovely butterflies are my daughters, Hope, Faith, and little Charity."

After swallowing hard, Christian said the first thing that came to mind. "Are you ladies the reason why this place is called the Palace Beautiful? Cuz never in my entire life have I seen ladies as fine as you all are."

The older ones shyly covered their mouths and giggled while Charity asked innocently, "Are you talkin' bout me too?"

Christian smiled and kneeled down to look into her eyes. "You, M'lady, are a true dime piece—the flyest one of all."

"You hear that, Mama? He said I'm a true dime piece! That means I'm a perfect ten and I'm only seven years old!" Charity said excitedly.

Discretion's attention focused on Christian, her tone serious. "Now it's gonna take more than charm to stay in the house of the King. This road you travelin' only gets rougher from here. There have been many pilgrims who stay the night here with strong spirits and hearts full of fire for the King, the way you are right now, only to have that flame put out by what awaits them on the other side of this palace. They think it's all gonna get easier from here on out. They don't quite understand the serious implications of their choice to turn away from the world and join the King. Are you ready to face a world that will be against you once you leave this place, Christian? Are you willin' to stand your ground against the Wicked Prince and his followers who will stop at nothing to keep you away from the Celestial City?"

Christian stood with his head held high and confidently answered, "Yes. I have been through many challenges that have caused others to turn back. Yet, I have pressed on with the hope that I will reunite with my grandfather and together we will be with the King. I do love the King."

Looking at him with a mother's adoration, Discretion smiled and hugged Christian tightly. "I'd love to hear about this grandfather of yours. He must be some kinda special to make you so sure that this is the right thing to do, but that will have to wait till morning. We gotta get you in bed so we can all get some rest. Welcome to the Palace Beautiful, Christian!"

Christian was very happy to stay there.

17

ARMOR

Thank You, King, for this bountiful feast that You have provided by Your good hand. Bless this food to our bodies for strength and nourishment. Thank You, too, for bringing us Christian. In Your precious Name . . ."

Everyone chimed in one voice, "Amen!" Christian loved hearing Hope talk. He could listen to her accent all day and never tire of its melodic sound. "Let's eat!"

Christian sat up straight in his chair and eagerly got his plate ready. He had slept well and he wasn't sure what he was most thankful for: the rest, the delicious breakfast spread before him of biscuits, gravy, eggs, and sausage, or meeting such wonderful friends. Having Faith sit next to him was a nice added bonus. He looked at her and smiled. She smiled back.

After everyone's plates were loaded with the mouthwatering food, Christian blurted out. "I have a question I've been wondering about." This family made him feel so comfortable, he felt like he could talk to them about anything! Besides he did have a lot of questions.

Truth looked at him, his forkful of eggs paused in midair. "What is it, Christian?"

Christian looked down embarrassed, second-guessing himself. He started, hesitantly. "Well . . . um. . . ."

Faith put her hand on his arm. "Ask, Christian. There's no such thing as a stupid question. Isn't that right, Mama?"

Discretion smiled. "That's right, Baby." Turning back to Christian, she asked gently, "What are you wonderin' about, Sugar?"

"Well, the Book says that once we do our ABCs . . . you know, A – admit we make wrong choices and can't make good choices on our own; B – believe in the King that He sent His own Son to die and free us from our burden so we can be with Him forever; and C – choose to live His way . . . we are always on the King's team."

Truth and Discretion both nodded proudly at his knowledge. Christian continued, his forehead wrinkling, "But, how do you *really* know?"

"Good question," Truth responded, putting his fork down to concentrate on the answer. "Let me see if I can answer that for you." He folded his hands and leaned back in his chair. "Lots of pilgrims ask that same question, Christian. Once you believe the ABCs in your heart and declare it with your mouth, you are on the King's team forever. See that scroll that you wear? That is the assurance of your salvation that you belong to the King. If you are not in too much of a hurry, you could stay here for a few more days. We could talk about it more and answer any other questions you may have. We would like that, wouldn't we, Family?" Discretion nodded, her eyes gleaming, and the girls squealed in excitement at the idea. When Christian agreed, Faith leaned over and gave him a quick hug.

After days of enjoyable conversation and fun times with the family, Christian awoke on the fourth day at the palace after a deep night's sleep to find Charity bouncing on his bed in excitement. "Wake up! Wake up, Christian! Wake up!" She shook his arm as he opened an eye. "Christian! Christian! Wake up! The King has a gift for you today! It's big!!!" Rubbing his eyes, Christian sat up slowly. "Okay. I'll be down. Gimme a minute." Charity skipped out of the room. "Mama, he's coming in a minute!"

The times spent at the palace were the most restful days Christian could remember in a long while and he wanted to stay in bed. Images from the many family conversations about life with the King, His Book, singing, and private walks played continually in his mind. Christian especially liked hearing the stories of the pilgrims who went before who stood against incredible odds, in the name of the King, and were triumphant with His help. One of Christian's favorite memories was when Charity eagerly pulled him over to a large oil painting on the wall in the study. Christian fell back on the fluffy down pillow and closed his eyes, letting that special moment vividly flood his mind.

"This is a picture of the Guard Angel, Chris, and each one of us gets to have one of our very own," exclaimed Charity happily.

"You mean, Guardian Angel," Faith said gently, correcting her little sister.

"Oh, yeah. That's right. The Guardian Angel."

Christian could see why Charity was so drawn to the picture. A boy was walking alone down a dark, narrow path. Close behind, a Shining One was holding a lantern in one hand, illuminating the next step on the path, with the other hand outstretched "to make sure the boy is caught if he falls," Charity had explained to him in a whisper. Under the painting were words from the King, which Faith had read aloud: "He will command His angels to take good care of you. They will lift you up in their hands."[1]

"Christian! Christian! Where are you? You need to come NOW!"

Charity's impatient voice jarred Christian back to the present. He stretched, yawned, and jumped down off the bed, hurrying to get dressed. After running down the stairs, he was warmly greeted in the grand foyer by all the ladies with a cheerful "Good morning, Christian!" His heart fluttered with excitement. *A big gift from the King? What could it be?* The excitement quickly turned to embarrassment when Faith whispered to him that his shirt was on backwards. He didn't care, though. His curiosity and anticipation overshadowed any embarrassment. Discretion wrapped him up in a warm embrace. "Christian, you are about to be given a valuable and most necessary gift. But first we have to put some meat on those bones, Sugar." And with a wink, she turned toward the kitchen. "Come on! Let's eat, Family!"

When all of them were sitting at the table with a feast spread before them, Charity looked around earnestly. "Is Papa comin', Mama? Is he going to eat with us?"

Discretion looked down at her youngest, lovingly. "No, Baby. Papa already ate. He got up early this morning to finish that special project he's been working on." She winked. "Now who would like to thank our King for our meal?"

"I will," Christian said, sliding in his chair just in time after fixing his shirt. He thanked the King for the meal and his new family.

He tried to eat quickly, but the butterflies in his stomach wouldn't let him. Faith seemed to sense his nervous excitement. "Wanna take a walk in the garden with me?"

The fragrant flowers and warm sunshine welcomed them outside. After moments of comfortable silence, Faith spoke quietly. "Do you ever miss home, Christian?"

Christian paused. He hadn't thought much about home these days. "Naw, not really. It had its nice things, but there was violence, arguments, gangs, and somethin' was missing.

But, I do miss my mama and my little sister. To tell you the truth, I feel more at home here in the Palace Beautiful than I ever did in D'City. I feel a peace here that I never felt before, not even with my mama. But Gramps, he was peace to me."

"Gramps must've meant a lot to you."

"Yeah, he sure did. He's the one who first told me about . . ."

"Faith! Papa and Mama are lookin' for you!" It was Charity, her face all aglow with excitement.

Faith looked into Christian's eyes and forced a smile. "It must be time, Christian," she said. "See that door over there?" She pointed to a solid wooden door with a golden handle. "Just go inside. Papa and Mama are waiting for you there. It's the armory where Papa works. I'll be there in a little bit. I want to talk with the King first." Faith squeezed his hand lovingly and Christian nodded, walking in the direction of the door.

"Woooaaahh!" Once he opened the door, Christian stared wide-eyed, his mouth gaping open in total amazement. Never before had he seen so many fascinating weapons and brand-new armor in one place!

Truth stopped his work at Christian's arrival, and taking off his welder's helmet, reached out his hand to Christian. "Welcome to the armory, Son. Is this place cool or what?" Christian nodded, still overwhelmed at the sight. "Go ahead and look around. I'll be there in a bit. Have just a little more work to do on this breastplate." Christian looked in the direction of

Truth's workspace. Metallic dust, mixed with dirt and grime, covered every inch of the workbench and tool rack. With the sight and sound of fiery sparks creating a masterpiece behind him, Christian turned to explore the wonder in the room.

All of the armor pieces were neatly arranged according to their various sizes—some so tiny, they could fit a small child! The warm glow of golden helmets caught his eye and he walked over to them. Picking one of them up and turning it from front to back, Christian marveled at its polished mirrored surface. Christian scrunched his nose up and stuck out his tongue, snickering at the distorted face that stared back at him. He stepped back. Along the bottom were rows of shoes and boots of assorted styles and colors. *Shoes for armor? Interesting.*

Silver and golden breastplates along with colorful shields bearing fancy designs of crosses and crowns lined the back wall. One shield, in particular, captured his attention, and Christian outlined its elaborate cross design with his finger. Maybe it was his gratitude from all he gained, but for some reason, he felt very drawn to the symbol of his freedom. He then walked over to the leather belts and many double-edged swords with decorated hilts, hanging in straight lines, their sheaths hiding deadly razor-sharp blades. The swords were too tempting. Taking one out of its protective sheath,

Christian began to swing it back and forth, amazed at how easily it sliced through the air.

"Hey! Be careful with that! That sword is dangerous!" Christian jumped at the unexpected voice. He didn't realize that Faith had just come into the armory. Embarrassed, he quickly put the sword back in its sheath and hung it in its place. She continued, "Amazing, isn't it? All of this armor is for the King's soldiers—finely handcrafted from the King Himself. It's the best armor ever."

"Really?"

"Really. He really loves His pilgrims and wants them to be protected. He's a good King." Tears welled in Faith's eyes as she looked at Christian. "I really don't know why He loves us so much. He loves us no matter how many times we fail Him. He is always, always there for us. That's why for all I trust Him."

"Christian. Come over here, Baby." Discretion was calling him over to where she, along with Charity and Hope, were standing in front of a sizeable wooden table. Christian smiled as he saw the image of him and Faith reflected in the large gilded mirror on the wall behind the ladies. Turning toward him with a sparkle in her eye while sweeping her hand across the table, Discretion said, "Christian, the King handmade this set of armor perfectly suited just for you."

Christian began to jump and shout excitedly, "Yes! My own set of armor! Do I get a sword too?" He looked toward Discretion, and their eyes met. His eyes were wide with wonder, hers solemn with the reality of what was to come. Truth walked toward them with the same solemn expression on his face. Christian looked at all of them suspiciously. The girls even seemed unexcited.

Hope spoke up with a soft serious tone. "This is not a fun costume, Christian. This armor is to protect you for the battle that lies ahead."

"Battle? What battle?"

"You will be facing the Wicked Prince and his minions on your journey, and the King wants to make sure that you are kept safe. The Wicked Prince and his minions want nothing else but to steal, kill, and destroy the King's pilgrims."

Christian's confusion vanished instantly, as fear and nervousness took its place. Faith encouraged him to put the armor on. "Don't worry. The King gives us gifts that are good for us. Go ahead. Try it on. It should fit you perfectly."

"Here, Christian." Charity held out a pair of black leather boots to him. "Put these on." Stepping forward, Hope offered him a small stool. "Sit here, Christian. These boots will never get old or wear out. But you must be ready to go wherever the King asks you to go and tell other people about His love." She unfastened his old, worn-out boots and laced up his brand-new ones, tying them securely. *Wow! They fit just like a glove and so comfortable!*

"One belt! Coming right up!" Charity interrupted his thoughts with her cheery voice. She handed him the black leather belt with a silver belt buckle, beaming. Christian accepted it, appreciating her loving helpfulness, and fastened it tightly around his waist. Discretion placed her hand on Christian's shoulder. "When you wear this belt, remember the King's truths. He is real, He loves you with a love that never stops, and He will keep you strong. The Wicked Prince, also known as the Father of Lies, will whisper untruths in your ear to get your focus off the King and His path. Always hold tight to what the King says. Keep those things in the forefront of your mind."

Next, Truth fastened the golden and silver breastplate around Christian, while Discretion explained its purpose. "This breastplate will guard your heart. Always do what is right, best, healthy, and good, Christian." He was surprised how weightless it felt, conforming perfectly to his upper body. *This is tripped out! How does the King know me so well? There are so many other soldiers for Him to worry about!*

When Faith handed him his shield, Christian gasped. It was exactly the same shield with the intricate cross and crown pattern that he liked above all the other shields. He reached out to grab it and was surprised at how light it was! "You make a handsome soldier, Christian. The King will always protect you. Remember what I always say . . ." Christian completed the sentence for her. ". . . For all I trust Him."

"This is the most important weapon you will ever have." Truth held a beautiful sword with a distinctive hilt out to him. As Christian reached out for it, Truth looked at him solemnly, his eyes reflecting the weapon's significance. "Christian, on the path to truly connecting with the King, the greatest battle we must all face as individuals is the battle with self. This sword contains the mighty power of the King's messages. It will defeat whatever enemy you face with the words that come from the King's mouth Himself."

Christian didn't quite understand, but he nodded and received the sword from Discretion. He caught a glimpse of himself in the mirror and turned to fully face the image of this new soldier. Pride and confidence, tinged with fear, reflected back. "You mean I gotta fight a grown man with this stuff? I have to really use this sword?" His voice cracked, exposing the fear that crept up from deep within. Truth placed a firm reassuring hand on Christian's shoulder. "Yes, Son. But the King's all-sufficient power is with you."

"One more piece of armor and perhaps the most important." As Discretion placed the helmet on his head, she blessed him. "With this helmet may you always remember, Christian, you forever belong to the King and nothing or no one can ever take you away from Him. You are His child forever."

Hope spoke next. "As you wear this armor, remember the King promised that He will help and protect all of His soldiers all the time. You will need to wear all of this armor at all times, though, and you'll be okay in whatever situation you find yourself. The King will always be with you. If you need Him, just call out to Him and He will answer."

Christian grasped the sword tighter and felt a surge of power rush through his veins, cutting through the fear and nervousness. He raised the sword up high. "I will fight with the King's help and power!"

Truth and Discretion smiled approvingly at his newfound confidence and bravery. "Come now, Christian. You are now well-rested, well-fed, and well-prepared. You are now ready to continue your journey."

The five of them walked to the front doors of the Palace Beautiful. "Thanks again for everything. I won't forget you!" Putting his sword and shield down, Christian meant every word as he wrapped his arms tightly around Discretion's waist. She had felt like a mom to him. "Group hug!" Truth, Faith, Hope, and Charity joined them in a big, warm, embrace not wanting to let Christian go. They had had so much fun together!

"Okay, girls. Christian must be on his way." Discretion smiled at Christian. "One more gift for you." Looking up at Truth, she spoke with her eyes. Understanding her request, Truth reached into his pocket and placed something in Discretion's outstretched hand. Fastening the golden chain around Christian's neck, she advised, "Keep this Key of Promise close to your heart, Christian. May it unlock doors that imprison you in darkness and bring you back into the light." Christian nodded feeling very confused at her words, but accepted the gift. "Now for your blessing." Discretion placed a hand on his helmet, her eyes shining with love. "Christian, baby. May you keep your eyes fixed on our good King. Be bold. Be strong. May you always remember how much He loves you. Go now, and know that the King is always with you and will fight for you."

"Thanks!" Christian gave Faith one last quick squeeze goodbye and picked up his sword and shield. After turning and waving goodbye to his new beloved family, Christian grasped his sword tightly and walked to the King's Path. Catching his gaze, Watchful waved to him and called out, "A pilgrim passed by here not too long ago. I think she said her name was Faithful. She was so focused on getting to the Celestial City and didn't stop. If you hurry, you can catch her so you won't walk alone. Godspeed, my friend!"

Christian waved back. *Faithful? The Goody Two-Shoes Faithful from D'City?* Caring not to think about her just now, he approached the lions at the palace gates. He paused. He felt no fear this time, standing in the middle of them. Breathing in deeply, Christian raised his sword heavenward. He felt invincible. Nothing could stop him now. Nothing.

....

[1] Psalm 91:11–12 NIV

18

BATTLE WITH SELF

Swoosh . . . Swoosh . . . Swoosh!

The sound of the air separating as Christian swung the sword from left to right made his heart race. The oversized hilt and long double-edged sword was weightless in his hands allowing him to strike swift and sure. His every move was precise and intentional. His technique was so fluid that it seemed as if he had been trained to fight with a sword his entire life.

Swoosh . . . Swoot, Swoot, Swoot . . . Swoosh!

Christian couldn't believe the connection he had to the sword. He could feel it guiding his movement. The sword, along with the rest of the armor, gave him a sense of power and confidence that he had never felt before. He felt invincible. He felt unbeatable. *Who can stop me as long as I have this sword in my hands? Who would dare to face me? Christian—loyal Knight to the King and Champion Defender of the Celestial City!*

The Wicked Prince, that's who!

Christian paused for a moment to allow this truth to sink in. This was not one of his video games, nor was he an innocent toddler with a tree branch in his hands pretending to be a knight of the round table. This was reality. The sword was real. The threat to his life was real! *Somewhere in this wilderness, there is a full-grown lunatic of a man, with a heart full of hate, waiting to confront me.* Christian knew the Wicked Prince would stop at nothing to end his journey.

Christian's last conversation he had with Faith came to mind. "There is no avoiding this battle, Chris. We all, who decide to follow the King, must face the Wicked Prince at some point in our lives. It will not be easy and he will show no mercy, for he is cruel and unjust. His heart is black as night and his eyes are ablaze with intense hatred." Faith paused, lifting Christian's chin so their eyes met. Smiling confidently, she continued, "Fear him not, Chris, for you are not alone in this battle to come. The King has already given you all that you will need to be victorious. He will not physically be on the battlefield with you, but through these very special gifts that He has given you, He will guide, protect, and fight alongside of you. Trust in Him, Chris, and you will surely get to the Celestial City. You'll see."

Her words filled Christian's heart with courage and hope as he leapt forward through the air, turning 360 degrees before bringing the sword down in a graceful, yet deadly, arc. Ting! Sparks flew as the sword sliced through a large boulder as if it was a stick of butter. Christian stared in awe at the two halves of the mighty stone, stunned that he had split it so easily. He lifted the blade and to his amazement, the sword had no signs of damage—not even one scratch!

Wow! I just . . . I mean, this sword just . . . Maaaaan! I just split a boulder in half with one swing. This sword is really something special! I ain't worried about nothing. Bring it, you crazy psycho. I'll be ready.

Placing the sword back into his sheath, he took a seat and grabbed the brown paper bag that he had gotten from Faith just before leaving the Palace Beautiful. She packed it herself with enough food to last him awhile. As he bit into the tasty sandwich, he began to think of her. He was definitely attracted to her. *Who wouldn't be? She is more than a dime piece.* But it was the way that she carried herself and her devotion to the King that made her so special to him.

Christian gazed into the sparkling water of a pond that was just a few yards from where he was sitting. The glimmering waters reminded him of her twinkling hazel eyes. *I guess I've got one more reason to reach the King and His kingdom. Yep. For the King, Gramps, my life, and now Faith, I would fight an army of evil princes!*

Christian decided to open the Book and read the first verse that he saw. He took the Book out of his cargo pants pocket and read aloud, "The Lord is my shepherd; I shall not want. He makes me to lie down in green pastures; He leads me beside the still waters. He restores my soul."[1] Surprised, he closed the Book and smiled. *This verse describes exactly what I'm doing!* He remembered Gramps telling him about how special the Book really was.

"You see, Son, this book isn't like any other book in existence. It is a map that shows us the ways of the King. It's a manual on proper livin' and a safety blanket in times of fear. But, what I love most about the Book is its wise counsel. There is nothing new under the sun, Chris. Everything happenin' today has been happenin' since the creation of the world and the Book tells us how the King would like for us to deal with life's many struggles. We are not smart enough to handle life on our own, even though all of us at some point think that we are. The good Book says that 'there is a way that seems right to a man, but its end is the way of death!'"[2]

KABLOOM!

Christian was thrown into the air before landing into the very pond that made him feel so at peace. He quickly pulled himself from the waters that served as an aqua net, breaking his fall. The wonderfully green and plush pasture that served as his resting place was now nothing more than a dark ash-filled crater. Horror filled his heart as he viewed the hole created by . . . what?

"Why do you ponder a question to which you already have the answer, boy?"

Every bone in Christian's body rattled with fear at the sound of that voice. That very same voice he had heard when he allowed himself to be misguided by Worldly Wise at the top of the hill. It was him, the one that he knew he must face, but hoped beyond all hope that he wouldn't have to. It was the Wicked Prince himself!

"Yeeees! That's right, boy. I am here to reclaim that which is rightfully mine, you! You belong to me! As are all who are born unto this world, anyone who tries to turn away from me shall most certainly be destroyed! Now turn and face your true master, boy!"

Christian's mind was racing. He had no idea what to do. As he began to turn and face his attacker he caught a glimpse of the Book, now singed and torn, lying next to his sword and shield. Maybe if he did a dive roll he could get to them and defend himself.

"If you think you're getting your sword and shield will help you, go ahead and get them. They will do you little good. Do you actually believe that slicing through the air and splitting rocks have made you into a warrior? Fool, the air and rocks do not fight back! If you so much as flinch in the direction of your precious gifts, I will take that as an act of war and I will snatch the life right out of you!"

Is he reading my mind?! How can he know what I want to do?! Oh, no, forget this, man! I better get to my weapons, cuz if I don't, I'm dead. Christian propelled himself forward with all the strength he could muster. He tucked, rolled, and

came out of his tuck, grabbing his sword and shield just as the ground around him exploded. It blew him back into the air, but this time though, he instinctively twisted his body in midflight and landed just in front of his assailant.

"Ohhh . . . my . . . King, help me!" The slimy, evil fire-eyed vision of the Wicked Prince was more terrifying up close than Christian had ever imagined. Standing at least eight feet tall, the Wicked Prince's body was massive and ripped. He wore an armored breast plate, burnt orange with blue tiger stripes along his ribcage. His serpentine eyes, ablaze with blue flame, could be seen through the cutouts of his helmet with horns of a bull lodged on each side of it. His brownish-grey skin, not covered by his armor, appeared to be more like the scales of a dragon, and he bore razor sharp teeth seen through his demonic smile. Smelling the fear growing within the child, the Wicked Prince extended his dragon-like wings and pounded the ground with his oversized weapon.

"This is the Dragon Scythe, boy, and it has taken the heads of many who have defied me. Think of how that pretty young thing, your little Faith, will feel once I have returned your helmet to the palace gates still filled with your severed head. Now! This is your last chance! Renounce the King and bow down to me . . . OR DIE!"

Christian looked all around him as a towering wall of blue flame encircled the two combatants, eliminating any chance for him to dart for cover. He was amazingly calm and he began to feel warm all over, the heat coming from the sword. *That's it!* He could feel the King's assurance as he prayed he would somehow survive this spiritual assault.

"I will never renounce my King! He is my rock and my salvation! You are nothing more than a cowardly beast with a bad case of dragon breath. I will never bow down to you!" Christian screamed as he readied himself for battle.

"I hope your sword is as sharp and swift as your tongue, boy. Humph!"

"Beast with dragon's breath!" challenged Christian. "Do your worst!"

"Sticks and stones, boy. Oh well, have it your way! I may not be the Burger King, but I definitely know how to flame broil!" yelled the Wicked Prince as he raised his left arm in the air.

Three balls of demonic blue flame materialized out of nowhere in front of the Wicked Prince before being hurled into Christian's direction. The fiery grenades were but a few inches and moments apart. Christian jumped to the right to avoid the first two explosive fireballs.

KABLOOM! KABLOOM!

The force of their impact was enough to knock Christian off of his feet. This left him wide open for the third ball of destruction. He only had a second to recover himself and brace for impact.

KABLOOM!

Christian was totally consumed by blue flame, earth, and smoke.

"It is done! It really is a shame how so many fools are led to believe that they can defeat me. If only they realized that I am eternal. That it was I who caused man to be exiled from that dreadfully boring garden to bring about death." The Wicked Prince stood over Christian's lifeless form and slowly raised the Dragon Scythe, bringing it down with relentless authority and twisted satisfaction.

Now! Christian thought as he rolled in toward the Wicked Prince, narrowly escaping the deadly blow of the Scythe. Christian quickly sliced his sword from left to right just above the Wicked Prince's belly button, penetrating the Wicked Prince's armor and slicing into his skin.

"ARRGH!" The Wicked Prince yelped as he grabbed his midsection in disbelief. Christian moved quickly to attempt another strike. Just as Christian lunged forward, the Wicked Prince jumped back out of reach of his thrust and instantly flew back into Christian with incredible force and speed. Christian leaned into his shield a second before the Wicked Prince rammed into him. Once again, getting knocked off balance before twisting in the air and landing on his feet.

The Wicked Prince swiped the Scythe from the ground and took flight. He was livid and wanted Christian dead. He had no idea how the boy survived the explosion, but he was going to make sure that the boy died a slow and painful death this time.

The Wicked Prince swooped down from the heavens with an over-the-head strike that would certainly split the boy in two. Christian moved out of the way at the last second and used his shield to ram the Wicked Prince. This wise move forced the Wicked Prince to reset himself before attempting another strike. Christian pressed on with a forward thrust of his own, which was barely blocked by the Prince.

Furious, the impatient Prince quickly attacked Christian with a flurry of attack combinations. Christian simply blocked and allowed himself to be pushed back, mindful to watch for a chance to land a clear strike on the now enraged Prince. The Prince twirled the Scythe and brought the blade in an under-over attack just as Christian spun out of reach, hoping to counter. The Prince, however, was able to use the momentum of his missed attack to bring the blade around his waist, catching Christian's shield dead center. Christian was not prepared for such a powerful blow. The wind was knocked right out of his chest as he soared through the air a great distance before landing hard on his back.

"You stupid little mongrel! Did you really think that you could defeat me? I started war! I am war! I know you inside and out. How? I am within you. I am Self, the reflection of sins past and the conductor of sins to come. I cannot be defeated, idiot! I am as eternal as sin itself!" The Wicked Prince screamed uncontrollably now, his anger greater than any level he had felt before.

That's it. Keep talking. Please keep on talking. I need time to get my bearings back.

The Prince continued. "You are chasing a myth. A dream, given to you by a silly old man who was nothing more than a fool himself! He planted a seed in your heart that has misled you! The King does not care about you! Where is your King now? Huh, where is He? I am the greatest force on this wretched planet! I am greater than your King and your grandfather who is now burning for all eternity in the fires of the underworld for his stupidity!"

"That is a lie! My grandfather was the wisest man to ever walk this planet!" Christian stood sure and confident, his body surrounded by a soft yellow glow as he stood to face the Prince of deception. The sword in his hand vibrated with power as he placed it atop his shield and settled into his battle stance. "He could not be in the flames of your underworld because his faith in the King was steady and true. My King created all things, including you. How can the creation be greater than the One who created it? You are the stupid idiot. You must be struck down!"

The offended Prince flew forward with even more speed and force than before. Christian stood his ground as the Wicked Prince struck his shield. The impact created a crater larger than all the previous ones combined. As the smoke cleared, Christian stood unmoved. The Wicked Prince was caught off guard with surprise and immediately started swinging the Scythe recklessly.

Christian blocked each swing with ease until finally the blade of the Scythe shattered against his shield. The Wicked Prince's eyes filled with dread and disbelief as he stared at his broken weapon. Christian found the opening he had been waiting for and plunged his blade deep into the stomach of the Wicked Prince.

"AURRRGH!!" The Wicked Prince screamed in astonished agony. With Christian still holding the hilt of the sword, the Prince slowly pulled the blade from his belly. Christian also yanked the sword toward himself with all the strength that he had, slicing deep into the hands of the Wicked Prince.

"AURRRGH!!" He screamed again as the blade cut through skin, muscle, and bone. The liquid that oozed from the wounds produced by Christian's blade was not blood, but the blackest unrefined oil Christian had ever seen. The Prince released the blade and ran into the forest, all the while vowing to get revenge. "You . . . fool! I cannot . . . die! Savor your victory today, boy. This isn't over!"

Christian lay down and looked into the cloudless sky. "Thanks King, for giving me what I needed and for not leaving me alone to face this psychopath. Faith and Gramps, I did it." Overwhelmed by emotion and fatigue, Christian lost consciousness.

....

[1] Psalm 23:1–3 NKJV; [2] Proverbs 14:12 NKJV

19

THE HAUNTED VALLEY

When Christian came to, daylight was quickly fading. He knew that in about an hour or two, darkness would soon settle around him. *How will I see my way then?* He looked around his surroundings seeking for someplace to rest. Trying to stand up, Christian felt woozy and quickly lost his balance, every bone and muscle in his body aching. *Whoa!* He remembered the scary battle where he almost lost his life. *I gotta get my strength back. I have to eat somethin'. Can't go on like this! King, help! I need strength.*

Christian took some time to settle his out-of-control emotions. *Go back to the crater.* He almost missed the still small voice, but he was sure he heard it. Struggling to walk back to that spot, Christian saw his shield lying in the black ash and . . . lo and behold! The sack of goodies from Faith was right where he left it! *Oh King, I hope it's still good. I need food.* He opened the bag, his hands shaking from hunger and anticipation. *Woohoo!* He fist-pumped his arm in the air and looked upward. "Thanks, King!" *Wow, the King even cares about a little bag lunch!*

After eating, Christian felt his strength return. *I'll just keep walking. Gotta be some place around to rest!* He continued on, noticing that the moon was hiding behind thick grey clouds. Suddenly, he stopped. The King's Path sloped downward as far as Christian could see into blackness. Black murky shadows hid any possibility of a resting place and he sure didn't feel safe. Turning back wasn't an option for him; he didn't want to face Self again. *There's only one way and that's to keep going.* He breathed a sigh of relief as the moon floated from behind its hiding place, illuminating the path in front of him with its soft glow. *Thanks, King. Now I can see at least a little bit.*

Christian swallowed hard, tightening his grip on his sword hilt. The path looked steeper than at first glance. *Faith said that for all I should trust Him. So, here I go.* Sliding down with pebbles rapidly cascading down in front of him, Christian leaned back to keep his balance, thankful for the sturdy traction from his thick black boots and protection from his armor.

Reaching the bottom of the valley, the lump in Christian's throat threatened to cut off all air to his lungs. This place looked scarier than any haunted house he'd ever visited. He squinted trying to see the path ahead of him, dim in the moonlight. Sharp rocks stretched out menacingly over his head over the path that appeared to be extremely narrow. *I'll be okay. It probably looks worse than it really is. With the moonlight, I'll be okay.* Slightly reassured, Christian walked forward putting one foot in front of the other, wishing there was another way. *Why do I have to go through this place?*

With each step deeper into the pitch-black valley, Christian noticed that the moon was playing hide-and-seek with him. *Not now. Please. I need the moonlight. I gotta see.* His skin exploded with goose bumps as he realized that he could barely see his hand in front of his face. He suddenly felt all alone. An inky mist began to settle around him bringing along with it eerie noises and painful wails. He covered his ears with his hands, trying to shut out the repulsive sounds.

Confusion began to cloud his mind causing thoughts to tumble through his head, like clothes in a dryer at the Laundromat. *This is crazy. I could die here! This doesn't make sense. Why would the King send me here?* He shook his head, as if shaking it would help him regain his focus. A ghost brushed by his face. Or did he imagine it? Christian began to shiver. His heart beat so fast and hard he thought it would explode right out of his chest.

Suddenly, flashes of lightning tore across the ominous sky. Christian's entire body now trembled with cold and fear. *What is this place?* Feelings of loneliness began to curl their ugly tentacles around Christian's mind again and suddenly, bone-chilling vulgar screams and the thud of footsteps filled the silence. *Sounds like the Wicked Prince's minions looking for someone. And I think they are coming toward me!* Christian froze. Fear consumed him and instinct took over. Holding his breath, he made himself as parallel to the slimy, cold rocky wall as his bulky armor would allow, trying to ignore the sticky mass of spider webs in front of his face. He silently hoped that its builder wasn't home. *Now if the moon will stay hidden and the lightning stays away so all this armor doesn't shine, I might be all right.* Christian heard the horrifying minions get closer. Just before he fell down from lack of breath, the voices and footsteps faded into the distance. He let out a gigantic breath, relieved. *They must've taken another path. Whew! That was close.*

Rubbing the webs from his face, he stood up again on the path. Taking a few more steps ahead, Christian wondered how long he would have to be in this haunted valley. He was very tired, but stopping was not an option. Ghostly voices slithered around his head taunting him, telling him to give up, to turn back. Lightning cracked overhead. He didn't know how much more of this he could take. Still scraping webs off his helmet, he kept determinedly walking forward step by step, hoping and praying for a break soon. Suddenly, a feeling of warmth enveloped him and he noticed that a soft glow illuminated his very next step. Christian gazed upward. The moon was still hiding, but when Christian kept putting one foot in front of the other, the small beam of light continued to remain just ahead of him. *I don't think that light is from the moon.* He paused and gasped. *Could it be? My guardian angel?!* Things didn't seem as spooky now, and he no longer felt alone. With new confidence, Christian continued on down the path into the blackness, surrounded by a powerful invisible protector.

"Even though I walk through the valley of the shadow of death . . ."[1] Christian paused for a second. *Wait a minute. I read those words before. And that was one of Gramps' favorite poems from the Book.* Christian thought he was imagining those calming familiar words, but they continued from an angelic voice. "I will fear no evil. For You are with me."[1] *Yes, Gramps used to say those words from memory. Mama recited them at Gramps' funeral. Truth, Discretion, and their girls mentioned them too.* Fond memories of his beloved Gramps, his mama, and his newfound family encouraged him onward. *For all I trust Him. All.*

Step by step, Christian continued onward. The words came echoing to him again from the same sweet voice. "... though I walk through the valley of the shadow of death..."[1] *That's gotta be Faithful. It sounds like her. Watchful said she was just ahead of me in the journey.* Christian smiled to himself. *Ms. Goody Two-Shoes. Always saying something about the King.* He remembered how he used to make fun of her strange outlook on life. But he was different now and having her to travel with, especially in this scary unknown place, would be nice. He wouldn't have to be alone. Christian strained to see ahead but the darkness hid the owner of the comforting voice from him. He wasn't sure how far ahead the pilgrim was, but he dared to call out. "Hey! Wait!"

"Hey! Hey! Wait! Wait!" Christian's voice echoed back to him, mockingly.

The voice stopped.

Christian continued, "If you're there, wait up! I'm a King's kid!"

"Wait up! Up! Up! King's kid! kid! kid!" Nothing but the empty echo seemed to laugh back at him.

Silence. And then the beautiful voice continued. "I will fear no evil; For You are with me."[1]

Christian walked faster to catch up. *King, is that really Faithful?* No sooner than the words were out of his mouth, when glorious brilliant rays of the morning sun crept over the horizon, casting light into the dark misty night. Christian relaxed. Night was over and day was beginning. The haunted valley was finally behind him. *Thanks, King.*

He paused. Ahead of him, dangerous nets and semi-hidden traps covered the King's Path as it sloped upward. He looked up to see a girl fade out of view over the top of the hill. Although he was anxious to catch up to the traveler, Christian focused on the path in front of him. He was thankful for the coming daylight. *The Wicked Prince sure pulls out all the stops to hurt the King's pilgrims!* He shivered to think what it would have been like if he had to cross this part in the dark. Stepping carefully, he slowly made his way up the steep hill.

Reaching the top, Christian saw the girl not too far ahead. He yelled out to her. "Hey! Wait up! We can walk together!"

The girl yelled back, but didn't stop. "I can't wait for you! I need to keep pressing on toward the Celestial City!"

Christian started jogging at an easy pace to catch up, but he was soon out of breath and had to stop. *Wow. Running in armor isn't like running with football equipment. That's for sure.* As he approached the girl, he noticed that it was Faithful. He was surprised to see that she was wearing clean clothes, but no armor. *That's kinda strange. I thought the King gives all of His pilgrims armor.* He caught up with her and extended his hand. "Hi, Faithful! Remember me from D'City? I'm Christian."

The girl smiled nervously at him, but shook his hand firmly. "Hi. Yes, I remember you, Christian." She looked back at the haunted valley that lay behind them and shuddered. "I'm glad that's behind us."

"Yeah. You and me both."

Faithful urged him forward. "C'mon, Christian, let's walk and talk. I want to get far away from this place."

You need to make things right with Faithful. Christian heard the voice in his head and knew it was right. He had called Faithful some mean hurtful words back in D'City and now was very sorry that he had said those things. "Uh, Faithful?"

"Yes, Christian?"

"Uh, I just wanted to apologize for calling you mean names back in D'City. I know now that was wrong. Will you forgive me?"

"Yes. Because the King has forgiven me of my wrong choices, I forgive you for yours."

"What can I do to make it better?"

"I know the King will change your heart to help you speak and act more like Him the more you spend time getting to know Him. I'm just happy I don't have to travel alone anymore. I'm grateful for your company, Christian."

Christian felt relieved inside. It felt good to be forgiven.

....

[1] Psalm 23:4 NKJV

20
TALKATIVE

"So when did you leave D'City?" Christian was surprised that he was actually walking and talking with Faithful. *Sure beats walking alone.* He smiled to himself. *Guess I've really changed a lot on this journey. I'm not the same person I used to be.* Back in D'City, he wouldn't have been caught dead hanging out with a Goody Two-Shoes.

"Oh, I left about three days after you did, Christian. I tried to catch up with you, but you left really quick."

Christian smiled a half smile. "Yeah, I guess I did. I just wanted to go. Hey, just wonderin', did you hear anything 'bout Pliable when he got back?"

"Yes. The whole block was talking about him. Poor Pliable's pants and shoes were covered in smelly goop. He was straight up mad for having his new shoes ruined. Lots of kids made fun of him for being a sissy and the guys in the Cool Crew gave him the cold shoulder. They fronted like they didn't even know him. I felt so sorry for him."

"Oh. Wow."

"I know. I wanted to ask him about you and encourage him at the same time, but every time I tried talking to him, he avoided me like the plague. Last I heard he just stayed to himself. He became a loner cuz nobody seemed to accept him anymore."

Christian was quiet for a few seconds and kicked the ground in frustration. "Man, I just wish there was somethin' I could've done, could've said, to make him stay with me. He's a cool guy. A follower, yeah, but he's cool."

Putting her hand on Christian's shoulder reassuringly, Faithful understood his emotion. "I know. It's so hard when people don't make the choices that are best for them. But we have to trust the King to help Pliable, Christian. Some things are not meant for us to do, no matter how hard we try."

"Hey, there! You two!" A whistle pierced the air coming from behind them. Startled, they both stopped simultaneously and looked to see an athletic-looking boy jogging to catch up to them. Christian turned to Faithful and whispered, "Where did *he* come from?" Faithful shrugged, her eyes narrowing suspiciously. "I dunno, but he kinda looks familiar."

The boy caught up with them, panting slightly. "Hey! Are you two going to the Celestial City?"

Christian spoke first. "Yeah, we are. You?"

The boy stood up tall and stuck his chest out. "Why, of course I am! Who wouldn't want to go and live in a mansion?"

Christian extended his hand. "I'm Christian. And this is Faithful."

The boy completed the handshake and nodded at Faithful. "Nice to meet you both. My name is Talkative. Mind if I walk with you? It's so much nicer having company than walking alone. Don't you agree?"

Faithful nodded her consent and Christian agreed. Just pausing enough to take a deep breath, Talkative kept talking, glancing back and forth between them as they walked. "Sure can't wait until I get to the Celestial City. Can you? Do you know what I heard about that place? It's not what you think it is." Seeing the surprised look on the two pilgrim's faces, he continued on arrogantly, pleased that he had their complete attention. "You know how you always hear about going to see the King in the Celestial City and the King this and the King that? Well, sure there'll be mansions, all the food you can eat, and paaarties . . ." Talkative rolled his neck and stirred the air with his arms in a dance, then paused for dramatic effect. "But the King really isn't there."

Faithful and Christian both stopped abruptly. "What?" Their shock and surprise made the word come out a little too loud. "Where did you hear *that?*" Faithful asked sarcastically as she glanced at Christian and rolled her eyes.

"For real! Duh! Everyone knows that! It's in the Book. Everyone that reads the Book should know that. It says that the King is not just in one place. He is everywhere." Talkative shook his head in disbelief at the two of them and sneered, "Man, I can't believe that you two actually thought you would meet the King Himself. That's impossible!" Before Christian or Faithful could respond, Talkative continued on, amusing himself. "Hmmph! Meeting the King would be like having it snow in the summer time or going up to the moon without a spaceship! Or . . . having money grow on trees! Or Antarctica turning into a desert! Or . . . touching your elbow with your tongue! Or . . ."

Christian interrupted his tirade. "Why don't you tell us about your journey so far, Talkative?"

"Wow! There's so much I could tell! I don't know where to begin! Well, I guess I'll start at the very beginning when I first heard that there really was a King." And without hardly pausing for breaths, Talkative began to describe his adventures, emphasizing his deep love for the King and his extensive knowledge of the words written in the Book. For at least the next fifteen minutes or so, Christian and Faithful could not get in a word even if they wanted to! Christian whispered in Faithful's ear, "Now we know where he got his name from." Faithful tried to hold back her giggle, but was unsuccessful in doing so.

Talkative was so preoccupied with himself that he didn't notice. He kept talking, "And then Evangelist . . ." He stopped. "Did you guys ever meet Evangelist? Guess you would have had to. Seems like everybody meets Evangelist somewhere, in some way. Well . . ." Talkative leaned in closer to the two, glanced around quickly, and putting a hand to his mouth he whispered, "You know, that old guy ain't who he really appears to be." Faithful and Christian's jaws dropped open at the same time in amazement. *Did he just say what I thought he said?* Christian mouthed the words to Faithful and understanding what he said, she shrugged. Out loud, she asked, "What do you mean, Talkative?"

Talkative smiled, pleased to be able to share the juicy news. "Well, everybody knows that he does what he does because he can't get to the Celestial City. The King doesn't want him there because he's been around the block, you know . . . The old guy's got a past. Word is he's never been married and has who knows how many kids running around and has done some, shall I say, underhanded stuff in his day. Word is he was locked up for a time over it." The stunned expressions on Christian's and Faithful's faces encouraged him to continue. "Man, I thought you knew. Everyone knows. People just like him and follow him because he's a likeable old guy, and his story is believable. Everyone wants to know that there is hope and something good to strive for. C'mon, though. You really believe that what he says is true? You really believe he's pointing people to the one place he can't even get to? He quotes words from the Book a lot and they sound good and all, but it was written by a bunch of crazy losers all back in old ancient times. Oh my gosh!" Something caught his attention. "Look at that. Did you see that?"

"What? See what?" Christian asked, his mind in a blur.

Talkative pointed. "That bird that just flew into the bush over there! I never saw anything like it before! Hold up. I want to investigate. I love birds, especially new species that

I never saw before. Be right back!" And with that, he jogged off to explore his new discovery.

"Whew!" Christian let out a breath. "He sure talks a lot!" Faithful laughed. "Guess he likes birds." Christian voiced his churning thoughts out loud. "Wow! He's trippin'! Where did he get all that from? It's weird, though. He seemed to know and love the King when he talked about his journey and he sure knows a lot about what the King's Book says. No wonder he's so confident he's getting into the Celestial . . ."

Faithful cut Christian off before he could finish, her eyes widening and her voice steady. "Christian, look. Maybe he can talk a good talk about the King and His words, but what about all that other silly stuff? Us going all the way to the Celestial City and not finding the King?" She put her hand on her hip for emphasis. "C'mon. You really think that's true? And the Book being made up of man-made stories from a bunch of crazies? And the lies about Evangelist? You gotta keep your head, Christian! He and people like him, just love to talk about anything and everything. That's all it is. Jibberish. You gotta believe the truth here," she pointed to Christian's head, "and here." She grabbed his hand to place it over his heart, her hand covering his. "And stand on it. Never let anyone tell you otherwise."

"I hear you, Faithful. I'm glad he's gone. He shouldn't be spreadin' those stories, especially hatin' on Evangelist like that. That can't be true." Christian glanced uneasily in the direction that Talkative went. "What if he catches up to us?"

Faithful wrapped her arm inside Christian's. "Let's just keep walking and see what happens. Besides, that bird might take awhile to catch up to." Giggling, they continued on together, enjoying the newfound silence. After taking a few steps in thoughtful silence, Faithful burst out loudly. "That's it! Now I know where I remember him from. From D'City. He was in the next higher grade than me at school. I never knew his name, but it's funny. I do remember him always talking."

"I don't remember him from school. Guess I was too focused on other things . . ." *like football and girls,* Christian finished the sentence in his mind. He cringed inwardly as he remembered how he almost let his greedy desire for fame and football keep him from the King.

"Anyone can say the right words, Christian, but I don't think the King's words have any meaning in Talkative's life. He seems confused. If he catches up with us, I guess we'll find out soon enough if he really does love the King or if he's just fakin'."

"How will we know?"

"Oh, we'll know. Trust me. The truth always comes to the light."

"Fweeeee!" A familiar whistle cut through the air. "Hey! Here I come!"

Christian turned to Faithful and rolled his eyes. "Well, whaddaya know. Here comes Talks-Too-Much."

Faithful tapped Christian's arm, "Be nice. The King loves him, too, you know."

Talkative caught up with the pair quickly. "Wow! You two missed out, I'm telling you! Do you want to hear what happened?" And without waiting for an answer, Talkative recounted his adventure of chasing a bird that had "rainbow-colored wings and a distinct birdcall unlike anyone ever heard before" in his life. "I tell you, I know I saw it. It was absolutely magnificent and unbelievable! Oh, and I saw a glimpse of this hairy creature, too. I love animals, you know. I don't know what kind of animal it was because it moved too fast and I couldn't catch up to it. Ooh, but it was hairy, I'm telling you! It reminded me of this girl, Alexis. The girl was so hairy that when she walked into a grocery store, the owner said, 'no dogs allowed!'" Talkative doubled over in laughter at his own joke, slapping his thighs.

Faithful sighed loudly, and changing the subject, she cast Christian a look that meant: *Ready for this?* "So, Talkative, do you *really* love the King?"

Quickly composing himself, he replied enthusiastically, "Oh yes! Oh yes! Oh my gosh! I love the King very much! He has been very good to me. I love being His pilgrim and doing all the things that He has asked me to do for Him."

Faithful continued, "Since you love the King then, I guess you are careful to obey *all* the King's rules?"

Talkative answered without hesitation. "Of course! All of them. Every single last one of them. That's the least I can do for all He's done for me."

"Oh, really?" Faithful's voice had a bite of sarcasm mixed with her everyday sweetness.

"Oh my gosh, yeah." Talkative's upbeat attitude quickly turned serious and he squinted at Faithful. "Duh! That's what I've been sayin'. Didn't you hear anything that I've been talkin' about?"

"Then why do you like to spread rumors and talk about people so much, thinking it's funny?"

Talkative's prideful tone turned angry. "Why you pressin' me? Everybody talks about people and what they hear. It's habit. But what I do or don't do is none of your business."

"I don't like it, and I know the King doesn't like it. Besides, if you truly love the King as much as you say you do, you would show it in both your words *and* your actions."

"What? How do you know? That's just what you think. You're just a girl—a Goody Two-Shoes."

Faithful turned to Christian and calmly asked to see the Book. Christian took it out of his pants pocket and handed it to her, curious. Opening it to the desired page, Faithful confidently read these words, "A good man out of the good treasure of his heart brings forth good; and an evil man out of the evil treasure of his heart brings forth evil. For out of the abundance of the heart his mouth speaks."[1] She looked at Talkative. "They are the King's Words, not mine or some crazy loser's words. They are from the King Himself. He says so. Both your words and actions will show whose team you really are on—the King's or the Wicked Prince's."

At her words, Talkative's face turned different shades of red, as he exploded. "Oh my gosh! You judgin' my love for the King over some words? I was tryin' to help you both. You ain't my boss. I thought you were nice travelling companions. Man, I'm wastin' my time with you both. I don't need you! Besides, you travel slow. You're slower than molasses. A snail could beat you both to the Celestial City!" And with that, Talkative ran off angrily ahead of them.

When he was out of sight, Christian turned to Faithful, his eyes wide. "Wow! I guess you were right. He sure is trippin'!"

Faithful nodded. "Eventually, everyone does show their true colors."

Christian laughed. "In different shades of red."

[1] Luke 6:45 NKJV

21
WARNING!

"**W**ait a minute." Christian stopped walking abruptly and grabbed Faithful's arm in a tight grip. "Is that who I think it is?"

Faithful jumped at the unexpected motion and slapped Christian on his arm. "What are you doing?" she questioned, noticing him squinting down the road as if trying to see something.

"Oh my bad, Faithful. It's just that. . . . It is! Oh wow!" And without saying more, Christian sprinted ahead down the road as fast as his armor would allow. Looking in the direction that Christian ran off in, Faithful saw a figure of a stocky bald man dressed in an overcoat coming toward them from across the plain. She was thankful for the distraction, but prayed that he would not be another Talkative. She was truly glad that he was gone. "Forgive me, King, for that thought, but that's the honest truth."

Faithful giggled when she saw Christian literally almost knock the elderly man off his feet as he ran to him and hugged him. *He's just like a little boy! I wonder who that man is.* As she walked through the knee-high grass toward the pair who were animatedly laughing and talking, Faithful thought he looked vaguely familiar. Christian noticed her approach, turning to her with a broad smile. "Faithful, I would like you to meet Evangelist. Evangelist, Faithful. Evangelist showed me the light of the Gate and started me on my journey." *So that's it. That explains Christian's great admiration for him and that's where I've seen him before! He's the preacher from that church on the corner.*

"So nice to meet you." Faithful warmly shook the elderly man's extended hand.

"The pleasure is all mine, I'm sure." A wide genuine smile accompanied his kind words. Turning to Christian, he continued, "So, you two must have had quite a lot of adventures! Let's sit down. I would love to hear all about your journey so far!" And without any hesitation, Evangelist removed his overcoat and before placing it on the grass for them to sit on, almost by magic, he took out some crackers, cheese, and bottles of water from its deep pockets. "Hungry?" Time passed quickly as Faithful and Christian recounted their adventures as Evangelist listened attentively.

"The King has been very good to you both. He will always be with you . . . even to the end of the world."

"So what is coming ahead of us on our journey? Do you know?" Christian asked cautiously.

Evangelist grew serious as he shuffled his sitting position to a more comfortable position. After gathering his thoughts for a few brief moments, he finally spoke. "That is why I have come. The King has sent me to give you a warning. A warning that you must heed closely."

Faithful felt a lump form in her throat. She did not like the tone she heard in Evangelist's voice. Looking over at Christian, his face wore an expression that she couldn't quite read. *Nervousness? Fear?*

Evangelist continued, looking both pilgrims in the eye and pointing down the road. "Down the path just ahead, you will come to a grand city full of splendor and every worldly luxury that a person could ever want. But beware of its entertaining appearance because the entire city belongs to the Wicked Prince. Many goodhearted pilgrims are tempted to stop their journey and stay there and party amidst all the enjoyment and pleasures found there. Do not be one of them."

"If it's so harmful, then why must we pass through it? Isn't there another way?" Faithful found her voice before Christian did, but Christian looked at her relieved she asked the same question that was on his mind.

Evangelist shook his head. "I'm afraid not. The Wicked Prince gave strict orders that the city, called Vanity Fair, would be built on both sides of the King's Path so that all pilgrims have to pass through it on their way to the Celestial City."

"So, what should we do?" Christian asked anxiously.

"Walk straight ahead on the path without looking to the right or the left. Keep to yourself and stay focused on the King. Whatever you do, don't stop to talk to any of the city folk or browse the shops with their beautiful things. Sometimes the city folk leave the King's pilgrims alone as they walk through the city, but sometimes they treat the pilgrims very cruelly."

Faithful's voice came out in a whisper. "What do you mean cruelly?" In D'City, she had endured hurtful name-calling from peers who identified her as a Goody Two-Shoes, Stuck Up, Lame, and Nerd. Because of being solid in her faith in the King, she had been laughed at and excluded at school. She couldn't even remember having a best friend and had to sit by herself at lunch too many times to count. *Is that what Evangelist meant by cruel?* Somehow she didn't think so. Her gut told her that school was nothing compared to Vanity Fair.

Evangelist leaned forward, his eyes glistening with moist tenderness for these two pilgrims and what lay ahead of them. "To be honest, it is not uncommon for the city folk to beat the pilgrims or throw them in jail. Sometimes, they have killed . . ." Faithful gasped, tears filling her eyes, "the pilgrims for not serving the Wicked Prince."

Christian stood up protectively, wielding his sword in the air. "I'll just fight them all! Don't worry at all, Faithful. I will protect you."

Although admiring Christian's courage, Evangelist shook his head, looking at him with kind eyes. "Sit down, Christian, and put the sword away. Many battles are fought with sword and cunning moves, it's true. But there are some battles that must be fought quietly standing still, obeying the King, and letting Him fight for you. This is one of those times. Remember, He is all-powerful and is always with you." Closing his eyes, Evangelist continued, "In this world, you will have many troubles, but take heart! I, the King, have overcome the world."[1] He opened his eyes. "Yes, sir. Words from the King Himself. True words. Words to remember. You have nothing to be afraid of, not even death."

"Not even death?" Christian and Faithful both echoed the words together, the scary "d" word coming out in a whisper.

"Not even death," Evangelist assured them. Noticing their pale faces, he continued, "Death is not the end for pilgrims who love the King and belong to Him."

Christian and Faithful looked at each other in shock and disbelief. "It's not?"

"No, it's not. For when a pilgrim dies, the King sends His Shining One to carry that pilgrim home to the Celestial City to live with the King forever where there is no trouble, pain, or crying."

"Oh!"

"So you see." Evangelist moved to his knees and then stood up. Reaching out his arms to help both Christian and Faithful up, he continued, "You have *nothing* to fear, not even death itself. As a matter of fact, it has been said that those who die are blessed because they are done with the struggles and hardships of life and enter peace and rest."[2] Daylight was fading fast. "I know you must go, but I wish to bless you first." Placing a hand on each of their shoulders, Evangelist blessed them, "Be strong and courageous. Do not be afraid; do not be discouraged, for the Lord your God will be with you wherever you go."[3] And after giving warm reassuring hugs, Evangelist left as quickly as he came.

Christian and Faithful stared at each other, temporarily paralyzed by numerous emotions. Faithful found her voice first. "I wonder how far the city is."

Shrugging his shoulders, Christian replied, "I don't know, but we should probably keep walking. We don't have much daylight left and I don't want to get to the city in total darkness."

Faith nodded in agreement and the two walked in silence. Words just didn't come.

After walking some distance, both Christian and Faithful gasped at the same time, glimpsing the bright lights of the city ahead of them. Faithful reached out and clutched Christian's hand. "Are you afraid, Christian?"

Christian tried his best to appear strong and confident for Faithful, even though he was beginning to feel fear and anxiety. "A little bit, Faithful. I'm not sure of what's gonna happen in this place. You?"

Her eyes moistened, but the tears did not spill over on her cheeks and her face remained calm, her voice steady. "I trust in the King and I know He will take care of us. He has never let us down." She paused and smiled, good-naturedly tapping him on his breastplate. "Besides, you have your armor."

Glancing at her with admiration at her spunk in the midst of this tense uncertain situation, Christian replied, "I really wish that you would have stayed at the Palace Beautiful so that you could have met Truth, Discretion, and their family. Then you would have received your own armor."

A squeeze from Faithful's hand pulled him back to reality. "I have the King and you. What else do I really need?"

Together, they walked on, repeating the King's promises and being thankful for each other, as the lights of Vanity Fair beckoned to them.

....

[1] John 16:33 NIV; [2] Isaiah 57:1–2; [3] Joshua 1:9 NIV

22
VANITY FAIR

"O . . . M . . . G!" Christian couldn't believe that his lips slipped and used the King's name in a disrespectful way, but he couldn't help himself. He stood frozen in shock and surprise, mesmerized at the sights before him. Colored lights lit up the night sky, like the dawning of the sun, racing in all directions across a vast array of signs on unique elaborate buildings, all intended to draw visitors into its doors like moths to a flame. Christian stared at a building the shape of a pyramid with a sphinx on both sides of it. The mouths of these stone mythological creatures opened every so often to release fireworks into the sky. There was a building in the shape of a famous palace built in India, another was made to look like the coliseums of Rome, and there was even a building with a roller coaster on its rooftop!

"We gotta visit that place before we leave, Faithful! Do you like roller coasters? I love roller coasters . . ."

Christian continued to talk and walk. The atmosphere of Vanity Fair was electrifying and full of life! Promises of fun and excitement in the air drew Christian in with every breath that he took. He couldn't think of anything else except experiencing all that Vanity Fair had to offer. In fact, he was so pumped up with thoughts of roller-coaster rides, games, and parties that he didn't notice poor Faithful who had become quiet and withdrawn.

Faithful did not and could not share in Christian's enthusiasm. This place made her feel very uneasy. What Christian saw as fun and exciting, she saw as distracting and destructive. What he saw as alluring and cool, she saw as dangerous and bad. She didn't notice Vanity Fair's beautiful array of lights and elaborate buildings. She saw only the people of Vanity Fair where there were men walking and holding hands with other men dressed as women, scantily clad women flaunting themselves and promising a good time to anyone who would listen. Faithful noticed exchanges of money and small packets being passed between some people as they walked by each other. She shuddered at the repulsiveness of it all.

"What's the matter, honey? You walkin' around like a little lost poodle and starin' at us like you ain't ever seen a woman befo'."

Faithful was so deep in thought that she didn't notice that she was staring into a pack of these ladies of the night. She was jarred back into focus by one very well-built black woman wearing a red dress and a blond wig. She was signaling to the rest of her pack to stop and take notice of Faithful as well.

"I'm sorry. I didn't mean to stare. I was just . . . well . . . all of this is just so overwhelming for me," Faithful murmured.

"Get a load of Miss Proper over here, would ya?" said another curvy woman whose sparkling blue dress barely covered her body. Her big blue eyes sparkled in the same way as her dress, and she wore a red wig that didn't quite look right on her. She continued mockingly, "I didn't mean to stare. Well, what did you mean to do? I mean, you got the same goods we got. They're a little underdeveloped but with enough money and the right plastic surgeon, you can have a package better than mine!" Everyone around started to laugh at this statement. Blue Eyes continued, "Or were you thinkin' about partying with the big girls?"

Faithful recoiled at this unwanted and unthinkable offer. She started to respond, but was cut off by the lady in red.

"You know that broke chick can't afford us! Just look at her generic hand-me-down clothes! Besides she's wound up so tight, even a blind man can see that she is pure as the driven snow! I bet she ain't even had her first kiss yet."

More laughter.

"Well honey, if that's true, c'mon over and pucker up!" said some well-dressed man whose puckered lips made him look like a catfish.

Faithful could not stay silent. "Stop it! Stop it all of you, please! What wrong have I done to you that you should talk to me that way? You consider yourselves to be beautiful, but who says? Look at you women who stroll around half-naked to gain the attention of men! Where is your dignity and your respect? Respect for yourselves, and for the King who created you. Your outside may be appealing to some, but it's

fake, and on the inside, you are all ugly, very ugly indeed!" Faithful screamed between her heavy sobs. She was now crying uncontrollably hoping the crowd would just leave her alone. Instead, they got uglier.

"Who do you think you are? Comin' into our town and judgin' us. Why do all you Book totin' suckas think that you can just come in here and force your little religion down our throats? Me, shoot, I got a good life here!" Several others voiced their agreement.

Faithful wasn't finished. "My heart aches for you even more if all of you have knowledge of the Book and our King and yet . . ."

Blue Eyes cut in, "Baby, we don't need your heart aching for us. Let it ache for yourself. A lot of us here know the crazy stories in that book, but they ain't true. Besides here, there's no bunch of rules to follow. We have an easy life, doing whatever we want, whenever we want. The Prince takes great care of us and gives us everything we need and want." Putting her hand on her curvy hip, she added with a wink, "That's why I made a deal with the Prince that guarantees these good looks forever."

Faithful spoke loudly and firm. "I know that my Redeemer lives and one day I shall stand before Him and He will count me as one of His own!"[1]

"Well, right now you will stand before me," said a large muscular man wearing a black and gold pinstriped suit. "And when I'm done with you, baby girl, I'll be your king." He grabbed Faithful with such force she knew that struggling to free herself would be a waste of time.

"Unhand her big guy or I'll be forced to run you through!" It was Christian's voice.

"Who the heck are you, little flea?"

Faithful's heart nearly leapt out her chest at the sight of Christian. He was standing confidently with sword in hand ready to save her.

"I'm just the guy with a pretty sharp blade in my hand. The very same blade that cut up your boss a few days ago, big fella. Now, I'd hate to ruin such a nice suit, but I promise you these are the last words that I am going to utter. Let...her... go...now!"

The large man smiled, and then released Faithful from his powerful grip. As Faithful ran to get behind the protection of Christian and his weapon, all the men in the crowd ran to stand beside the very large man who didn't seem to be worried about Christian at all.

"You see you're more foolish than you look. Drop the sword now, or you and the girl will die now. Idiot, didn't yo' momma ever tell you not to bring a knife to a gunfight? Now drop your weapon before we have to bust a cap in yo' hide, boy!"

Christian looked all around and saw nothing but gun barrels pointed at them. He looked at his sword and then at Faithful. "Chris, it's okay." Faithful lowered Christian's arm and gently took the sword out of his hand. "The King will deliver us one way or the other. This is a battle you cannot win. Don't foolishly give up your life for me."

Christian sighed, glancing at Faithful. "I am so sorry. I should've been there for you from the start, but I got so caught up by all the theatrics of this place."

"No apology needed, Chris."

The crowd rushed the two of them quickly. People took turns punching and spitting on them as they bound and gagged them.

"Don't mess them up too much now. The Prince has made special plans for these two! Take them before Judge Haterade!" barked the large guy running the show. He stood in front of Christian and slapped him so hard his eyes started to water. The crowd cheered as Christian and Faithful were lifted by the angry mob and carried to an almost certain doom.

....

[1] Job 19:25 NIV

23

JUDGE HATERADE

Walk faster, Slowpokes!" The cruel guard yelled unmercifully at Christian and Faithful as they were being led, in handcuffs and ankle chains, to the courtroom of Vanity Fair. The judge had wanted to hear their case immediately, since he was extremely interested to see the two young pilgrims who had caused such a great disturbance in the city. The thick mahogany door to the courtroom opened and the two were rudely escorted to the front.

The courtroom was noticeably empty, except for an overweight man in uniform, his buttons bursting at the seams. He was sitting on a wooden chair at the front of the room, eating a chocolate-covered donut and looking very sleepy, completely oblivious to the new visitors.

"Aa-hem." The guard loudly cleared his throat to get his attention.

The large man looked up and stood, his face darkening to crimson. He rang a small bell that was on the wall behind him and in a deep baritone voice, he bellowed to an invisible courtroom audience, "All rise, Superior Court of Vanity Fair. The Honorable Judge Haterade presiding. Court is now in session. Please be seated and come to order." As if on command, the side door opened and the judge, clothed in an intricately embroidered black robe, entered the courtroom.

Sitting commandingly at the front of the grand room behind the large raised bench, the judge peered over wire-rimmed spectacles at the two youth standing before him. This was his moment of tremendous enjoyment pretending to be fair and listen to their case, but having the sheer power to punish them however he wanted, since he could and no one would question his actions. After all, the Wicked Prince had promoted him as the Judge and he would make sure he didn't disappoint his master.

"Tell me, who are you?" The words came out cold and heartless.

His heart threatening to beat out of his chest and knees shaking, Christian spoke first to protect Faithful. "We are pilgrims on our way to the Celestial City, Sir."

"Is that so, boy?" Judge Haterade sneered, his mouth twisting in cruel hatred. "Then why did you disrupt the peace in our city?"

Christian was silent.

"Speak, boy!" The coldhearted words echoed off the empty courtroom walls causing an icy chill to settle over the room.

In a nearly inaudible shaky voice, Christian answered him, "We didn't mean to, Sir. We were just passing through, minding our own business, Sir."

"Humph." In a mocking, sneering tone, he mimicked Christian's words, "We were minding our own business, Sir."

Judge Haterade leaned forward in his chair, his eyes squinting in a sinister glare. "Well, I don't believe you. The ruckus that you caused on your arrival to our city is inexcusable and will not be tolerated. Both of you deserve to be punished severely for it."

Looking at his watch, the judge turned to the guard who escorted them in. "It's getting late. Tomorrow, we will assemble the jury and hear their case. In the meantime, give them lashes; ten for the boy and half that for the girl. Beat them in the center of Solomon's Colonnade so all can see what will happen to those who disturb the peace in this magnificent city and think themselves greater than us." The gavel pounded loudly on the podium, punctuating the words of the pilgrims' harsh sentence. "Court is adjourned until tomorrow." And with a faint malicious laugh, Judge Haterade stood up and left the courtroom.

Christian looked over at Faithful, but before he could say anything, the guard yanked their chains unmercifully. "Walk, you fools! We don't have all night!" Obediently and without a word, Christian and Faithful were led like convicted criminals out of the courtroom to Solomon's Colonnade toward two guards who were eagerly waiting for them with belts in hand. In the moonlight, a crowd was growing rapidly, anxiously awaiting the amusing spectacle of the poor pilgrims. Solomon's Colonnade, an outdoor cemented area just outside the courthouse, was surrounded by massive white marble pillars. It was the site where pilgrims were often punished publicly. Out of mockery, the Wicked Prince purposefully ordered that the place be named that since, in the Book, the King's followers gathered in a place of the same name to worship their King.

Christian felt dazed as if he was living a nightmare, and wished with all his might he would wake up. One of the guards took great delight in tearing off Christian's armor piece by piece, laughing in wicked delight as he did so. But the first lash of the belt and the crowd's mocking roar told Christian this was no dream. "Where is your Beloved King now? Let Him come down and save you!" Whap. Whap.

Whap. Whap. Whap.

Christian looked over at Faithful. Her face was turned upward and although her skin was pale, it shone as if an invisible power illuminated her from within. Although her lower lip quivered and her eyes were moist, Faithful stood firm as she endured her specified lashes. The crowd continued to yell taunts and ridicules and at the sound of each lash, their mocking voices grew louder and louder.

Whap. Whap.

"Where is your supposed King now if He loves you so much?" "Yeah, some kind of a King He is."

Whap.

"Must feel real good serving your King!"

"Go ahead—say something!"

Whap.

Christian and Faithful remained silent.

Whap.

After the last lash, the guards shrank back in the shadows, satisfied over their work. Weak from extreme pain and exhaustion, Christian and Faithful lay bleeding and handcuffed on the cement, thankful for its nighttime coolness that provided some relief.

"We'll be okay, Christian," Faithful whispered. "The King really is with us. He will never leave."

Christian managed a weak smile. "Are they leaving us out here for the night?"

As if on cue, a male voice yelled out from the crowd. "These pilgrims are so young! They don't deserve this!"

And a sympathetic woman's voice. "They need a bed for the night!"

Another male voice. "And medical attention!"

A young innocent voice. "What did they do wrong?"

The voices were met with loud "boos" from the jeering crowd.

"Give 'em some more!"

"They deserve it!"

The taunts got louder and louder, and soon a fight broke out. Guards immediately came on the scene and broke it up just as quickly as it began.

"Hey! Hey! Hey! Who started this?"

An unkind voice shouted, "It was those two!" Several voices joined in the lie, "Yeah, those two pilgrims started it!" Fingers pointed at the wounded, hurting pilgrims, lying huddled together on the ground.

Without question, the main guard snapped the belt in his hand. "Causing more trouble, are you two? Guess the first round wasn't enough for you both." And with that, he gave both pilgrims three more lashes each. The crowd roared with delight, but the guards didn't want further trouble. Yelling into the crowd, they commanded, "Go on home. It's late. We'll continue this tomorrow." With some force, the unwilling crowd dispersed, mumbling and laughing as they went home.

The guards seized Christian and Faithful and dragged them heartlessly inside to a jail cell smelling of mold, urine, and human waste. Faithful gagged, and Christian managed to put his shirt over his nose and mouth to keep as much of the smell out as he could. Closing the door with force and locking it securely, the guards laughed. "Sleep tight, children! See you tomorrow!"

Christian and Faithful hardly slept that night in the pitch blackness, their bodies racked with excruciating pain. The sickening smell and the occasional scurry of rats didn't help either. But they both found comfort in talking about the King and His promises. Faithful spoke quietly into the darkness. "You know, Christian, there's really nothing to be afraid of. If we die here, we'll be carried to our home in the Celestial City."

Bright rays of morning sun streamed through the small window opening, signaling the start of another day. Christian stretched out his sore body as much as the handcuffs and ankle chains would allow. *Help us, King.* He glanced over at Faithful, finally sleeping peacefully. His heart ached for her.

Minutes later, Christian heard heavy footsteps and evil laughter coming toward them as two guards appeared. "Good morning! Rise and shine! Time for more fun!" Opening the door, one of the guards kicked Faithful in the ribs to awaken her. "Wake up, Sunshine! We gotta get going! Judge Haterade would love to see both of you fine pilgrims again today!" Christian and Faithful soon found themselves being forced again back into the hostile, cold courtroom. This time, the courtroom was packed with curious bloodthirsty onlookers, eager to hear the punishment of the hated pilgrims.

The same overweight uniformed man was sitting in his wooden chair, this time eating a donut covered in powdered sugar. When the guards and pilgrims appeared, he cleared his throat, rang the small bell, and in his deep voice bellowed, "All rise, Superior Court of Vanity Fair. The Honorable Judge Haterade presiding. Court is now in session. Please be seated and come to order." The side door opened and Judge Haterade entered the courtroom. Nodding to the jury of twelve people, he sat down at the bench. Still weak from their beating, Christian and Faithful were granted permission to sit before the judge. The audience loudly murmured their dissatisfaction.

"Order in the court!" Judge Haterade pounded his gavel. The audience grew hushed.

Judge Haterade spoke. "Well, well. My two pilgrims are back to see me." His mouth curled in an evil smirk. "Today, the jury will listen to your case to decide your fate. But before we begin, remind me. What are your names?"

Christian spoke. "I am Christian, Sir, and this is Faithful."

"Where did you come from?"

Christian answered, "We came from the City of Destruction, called D'City, and are on our way to see the King in the Celestial City."

Judge Haterade tried to keep his elevated emotions under control. Oh, how he hated—loathed the King and His followers. Peering at the unsuspecting pilgrims through his wire-rimmed spectacles, his eyes narrowed. "So, what you're saying is that you *pretend*," his voice emphasizing the word in obvious mockery, "to know and follow a better King than ours and are going to a city that you *pretend* is finer than this one?" His voice cracked with seething hatred. The audience didn't dare make a sound. Tension filled the air.

Christian nodded slowly, but Faithful could be quiet no longer. Ignoring her pain-filled body, she stood up filled with strength, power, and passion, her voice strong and steady. "Excuse me, Judge, but I need to speak. I cannot be quiet any longer." She continued on boldly, ignoring everyone's stunned expressions of such open defiance.

"Yes, Christian and I belong steadfastly to the King. He is the only way! Salvation is found in no one else, for there is no other name under heaven given to mankind by which we must be saved.[1] We must obey the King rather than the worldly pleasures of this place and others like it." Faithful's voice grew more confident. "The Wicked Prince only wants to steal, kill and destroy, but the King has come to give life abundantly.[2] Of course, the Prince won't tell you that, because he is the Master Deceiver and the Father of Lies."

At this, the audience and jury shouted in protest. "Blasphemy!" "Kill her!" Judge Haterade pounded his gavel. "Order in the court! Order in the court!" Christian sat, his mind reeling with the events going on around him. He admired Faithful's courage, but she needed to be quiet. He could sense the wickedness and anger that was increasing in the room with every word she spoke. He tried to get her attention to get her to stop talking.

Faithful continued on steadfastly, speaking now to everyone in the room. "Listen to my words! The King is the only Way and He loves with an everlasting love. He has defeated the Wicked Prince once and for all and wants everyone to come to Him. Choose for yourselves this day who you will serve, but as for me and Christian, we will serve the King!"[3] At this, the audience roared their disapproval at her words.

"Order in the court! I said, order in the court!" Judge Haterade shouted over the gavel's loud strikes.

Waiting until the audience was quiet, he looked over at the jury, his face red and his body shaking with fury. "You have heard the case of these two. What is your response?"

Without hesitation, the jury spokesperson stood up and addressed the judge and courtroom audience. "Judge Haterade, Your Honor, I am confident that I speak on behalf of everyone here. We do not need to talk this case over. It has already been decided. It is obvious that both of these pilgrims are wrong for disturbing the peace and fun here in our city. However, Faithful is a very stupid girl. She doesn't know when to keep her mouth shut." The audience murmured their agreement.

"Because she has spoken bold-faced lies about our beloved Prince, her punishment is death. Death by fire!" The audience clapped their hands and roared in delight and approval. He finished, "And for Christian, he can go to his pretend city and fake King after receiving five more lashes. And after the judge gives him permission to leave." Judge Haterade seemed pleased with this and pounded the gavel ending the court session. The overweight man stood and yelled, "All rise!"

Christian gasped. *Faithful, put to death? No! It couldn't be.* He shook his head, hoping he hadn't heard right. The noise in the courtroom was deafening and chaos erupted. The guards quickly grabbed Christian and Faithful, forcing them through a side door to avoid the angry mob. Being pulled through the crowd to the center of Solomon's Colonnade, Christian noticed a pole had been set up, with firewood around the bottom. A guard was pouring a strong smelling liquid substance all over the wood, saturating it. Christian looked at Faithful, tears streaming down his face. "I'm sorry, Faithful" was all he could say.

Faithful smiled. "I'm going home, Christian. It's okay. Keep following the King. And . . . I love you."

As she was forcefully yanked and tied to the pole in the midst of the chaotic screaming, Faithful remained peaceful and did not resist. Her face, turned heavenward, was brightly

Her face was brightly illuminated like the face of an angel.

illuminated like the face of an angel. And as the fatal match was lit, she cried out, "Father, forgive them for they know not what they are doing![4] Do not hold this sin against them. Oh King, receive my spirit!"

As tears streamed down his face, Christian looked up at the sky and saw a bright Shining One with wings outstretched, ready to carry his friend, Faithful, home to the King and the Celestial City. Weary from pain, exhaustion, and the events of the day, he fainted.

....

[1] Acts 4:12 NIV; [2] John 10:10; [3] Joshua 24:15 NIV; [4] Luke 23:34

24
HOPEFUL

"Arrrgh."** A low deep moan escaped Christian's lips as he tried to stretch his aching muscles. His whole body was throbbing with excruciating pain. His muscles and bones felt on fire. Opening his bruised eyes, he squinted into the bright light around him, trying to make sense of his surroundings. *Where am I?*

"You're awake! Oh! How are you feeling?" A gentle angelic voice welcomed him from his sleep. A soft hand rested on his forehead, as if feeling his temperature. "You don't feel on fire anymore. That's a good sign." The hand and voice belonged to a young woman, appearing to be about his age, who was sitting next to his bed on a small stool. Her ebony hair hung straight down her back, and her gleaming chestnut eyes and wide beautiful smile caught Christian's attention immediately. She smelled of warm vanilla and wore a formfitting fashionable outfit that accentuated her curvy young figure.

Christian closed his eyes again. *This girl looks hot! Am I dreaming?*

"I know your body must be really hurting. Those people were tripped out. They shouldn't have beat you and that girl like that. I'm so sorry." The soft hand pressed gently on his upper arm in sympathy.

Desperately wanting to know where he was, Christian mouthed the words, "Where am I?", but no sound came out of his parched lips.

Sensing his thirst, the young woman held a cup of cool water to Christian's mouth. It was so refreshing! He forced his muscles to curve in a small thankful smile.

"Where am I?" His voice cracked, while his eyes were now fully focused on the gorgeous girl next to him.

"You're safe now. I made my daddy pinky swear it. My name is Allure, and my daddy is in charge of the prison here in the city. After seeing you get your last five lashes, I begged him to let you stay here in the prison on a comfortable bed. I felt so sorry for you. It was wrong of them to set your friend on fire. Something she said must've really made them mad. I never saw those people that mean."

Christian's eyes filled with tears at the mention of Faithful. Just then, memories of the previous days came flooding back and he remembered. Judge Haterade. The cruel guards. The belt lashes. Faithful's calm. Name-calling. Evil laughs. The flames. "Forgive them." The Shining One.

Christian's eyes met her compassionate gaze and an instant warmth flooded his body. "Thank you for taking care of me." He said. He couldn't imagine where he would be now if she didn't come and help him.

Allure stretched out her hand, covering his. "It's the least I could do. Big Mama helped me. We found medicine and Band-Aids and did the best we could to clean and bandage your wounds and help lessen the pain. Big Mama and I were worried about you, but you sure took those whuppings like a man!" She squeezed his hand admirably and then quickly drew it away as he winced. "Oh, I'm so sorry! I didn't mean to hurt you!"

Christian just wanted this agonizing pain to vanish. He remembered that Evangelist told him that the King said that he would suffer, but he didn't know that suffering meant being beaten within an inch of his life! Faithful's last words to him were to keep following the King. *But sometimes following the King makes no sense.* He closed his eyes for a brief moment and prayed the only words that came to mind. *King, help me.*

Allure's sweet voice drew him to the present. "You know, Christian, you should stay here. Stay here in Vanity Fair at least until you feel better. I think you'll really like it here."

Christian shook his head side to side. The roller coasters, games, and parties didn't seem appealing any more. "I can't. I gotta get to the Celestial City. I have to see the King." *And Faithful. And Gramps.*

"And give this place up? Boys that come through here claiming to belong to the King always have big dreams like that. Look, Christian. Your friend is gone. That's a heavy burden you will always have to bear. If you stay here, we could hang out. I have a feeling that we could become really good friends! Please—just stay here! And soon, you'll forget all about her and the King's City."

Christian didn't like the sound of those words. *Forget about Faithful? Never!* She had been such a help and encouragement to him with her comforting presence and reassuring words. He was a better pilgrim because of her. Suddenly, without warning, the quiet hissing voice returned. *So, Christian, if Faithful was all that to you, how are you going to make it alone without her now?*

The thought paralyzed Christian. He hadn't even thought of that. The hissing voice continued relentlessly. *Maybe Allure is right. How can the King really love you? He took away your new best friend! How is that love?* Tossing and turning about trying to get comfortable and shake off the unnerving feelings and silence the voice, Christian caught a glimpse of something shiny in the corner of the room. Turning his head around completely, he noticed his armor lay there, and although most of the shine was gone, it was all there! Instantly, the taunting voice was silenced by joy, clear memories of the King's constant presence and help, and Evangelist's words, "The King is all-powerful and is always with you. In this world, you will have many troubles, but take heart! I, the King, have overcome the world!"[1]

Allure sensed the mixture of emotions churning within Christian and noticed him looking over at his armor. Gently, she placed her hand on his arm. As if she could read his thoughts and questions, she spoke. "Big Mama and I thought you might like your armor. We went back when the crowds left. I guess the guards forgot about it—I didn't think we would find it all, especially not the sword and shield."

Christian smiled at her. "Thank you." Struggling, he forced his weary aching body to sit up in bed. After accepting another drink of water from Allure, his face grew serious. "You know, I can't stay here, Allure. I love the King too much and I know He loves me. I have to go to Him."

Allure's beautiful wide smile quickly turned into a frown. "I just don't get people like you. You can have it all here, but you choose the lonely difficult way." She paused, observing his bandages. "But, you're not well enough to travel. It will probably take a few days for you to be strong enough. Maybe then, you'll change your mind."

A week later, Christian woke up to find a mysterious letter on the floor. *Someone must have slid it under the door during the night.* Although still very sore and bruised, Christian was able to walk around, thanks to Allure's tender care from the last few days and the King's healing touch. Opening the envelope, Christian gasped and pumped his fist in happiness! "Yes! Boo-yah! Thanks, King!" Judge Haterade had given permission for him to be freed.

Dressing hurriedly in his armor, Christian was determined to leave quickly. He appreciated Allure's care and felt bad that he wouldn't be saying goodbye to her, but his mind was made up. *I can't put myself in a situation where I can be talked out of it or held up. I gotta keep my focus on the King.* Christian shuffled down the street toward the outskirts of the city, his determination to leave overshadowing the pain in every step he took. People stopped and stared at him, whispering as he walked past, but no one bothered him. He mumbled a prayer of thanks. He just wanted to get out of this place and never see it again.

Just as he left the city limits and breathed a sigh of relief at the King's Path that lay before him, Christian heard fast approaching footsteps behind him. His sigh of relief turned into a sigh of frustration. *Not again, King. I just wanna get out of here and on my way again.*

"Hey! Yo, Chris! Wait up!" The voice sounded vaguely familiar to Christian. He stopped and hesitantly looked back. Christian blinked twice to check his eyesight. *Is that who I think it is? Naw, it can't be.* The boy was wearing a scroll cylinder similar to Christian's.

"Chris! Wait! Let me come with you!" The boy quickly caught up to Christian.

"Hopeful?! Is that really you?" *Hopeful a pilgrim?!* Christian looked at him skeptically, remembering the last time

Hopeful wanted Christian to go with him. *Jasi and Tina*. He smiled. *Wonder how they're doing*. Those days seemed long gone. A new life lay ahead of him and he wasn't about to let anyone or anything stand in his way.

"Yeah, man. It's me!" Greeting Christian with their old customary handshake, he continued, "It's been awhile! Didn't expect to meet up again like this! How you feelin, man?" He looked Christian up and down with concern. "They tore you up real good back there."

"Sore, but alive and thankful." Christian turned his attention to Hopeful. "So what you doin' *here?*"

Hopeful answered with hesitation, "I know. Weird, right? After you left, the Cool Crew got all crazy. Man, Obstinate got shot. Drive-by. Just like that he was gone. I wanted out of that scene with the girls and football. For a while they were fun. Man, I was livin' it up! But there was this emptiness inside that kept gnawing at me. I wondered if there was more to life, you know? So, one day I met a guy named Evangelist and what he said made a lot of sense. I knew that he had the answer that I was looking for. I left the next day. I couldn't wait."

"Wow! Good for you, man! Best decision you could've ever made!" Christian good-naturedly tapped him on his shoulder. "How long were you in Vanity Fair?"

Hopeful's face turned downcast. "For a minute."

"What happened?"

"Got sidetracked, I guess. It was a tough journey. When I got here, I was tired and very lonely. Started missin' my old life where I could do what I wanted. Reading the Book got dull. I wasn't gettin' anything out of it. Seemed like a waste of time. Started doubtin' if the King was even the way to go. Coming here, everyone was so friendly and welcoming. Life suddenly became fun again! I met these girls, Fortune, Blazin', and Easy. Man, talkin' about hot! They just got me, you know what I mean? They were the total package, man. Drop-dead gorgeous, rich, nice, easy to talk with and hang out with. Took my mind off things that were stressin' me. Like an oasis in the middle of the desert, you know what I mean? I didn't want to leave. I needed it like I need air to breathe."

"If you left D'City after me, I wonder why I didn't run into you on the journey. We could've traveled together. You would've gotten to know Faithful. To me, she was what every girl should want to be. She was the real deal."

"Yeah, sorry about your friend, man. I saw everything that went down back there. She seemed like she really loved the King. Didn't even fight back. Wait a minute—was she the girl from D'City that we all made fun of—Ms. Goody Two-Shoes?"

"Yep. That was her. She was awesome. Helped me out a lot." Christian kicked an imaginary pebble on the ground. "I miss her."

Hopeful was gonna roast him for falling for a Ms. Goody Two-Shoes, but then stopped himself. *I'm different now. I'm not that Hopeful anymore.* Instead, he said, "I thought she looked familiar. Well, when I left D'City, I left and I didn't stop. I didn't stop at any of the houses or that big palace that a lot of people talked about. I just wanted to get to the Celestial City. That's probably why I didn't see you. Anyway, I want out of this place. I want to get back to my journey."

"Why? What happened?"

"It's just like the same ol' thing again, man. Just like girls and football were back in D'City. Fun for a while, a good break from the daily struggle of life but man, it got old. The gnawing feeling came back and wouldn't let up. I feel like I'm doing it all wrong and I need to get back to the King's Way. That was the only time I felt true peace deep inside."

Christian nudged Hopeful on his back. "I'm proud of you, bro! I am finding that the King's Way is the only way, the best way. C'mon! Let's get far away from this city. It'll be fun travelling with you!"

Hopeful breathed out a sigh. "Thanks for givin' me another chance, man. I know I didn't treat you the best in D'City."

"No prob, bro! That's part of life, right? Grace is a wonderful thing." He paused. "Wouldn't it be cool, though, if we had a football to play catch with?"

"I thought you were still sore!"

"Can never be too sore for football!" And with a laugh, the two boys walked down the King's Path talking about old favorite football memories.

....

[1] John 16:33 NIV

25

VALLEY OF PEACE

"**M**an, you sure you okay?" Hopeful glanced over at Christian with uncertainty and concern. Putting an arm instinctively around Christian's shoulders, he continued, "Man, I know you are determined to get to the Celestial City, but don't kill yourself." Walking unsteadily, Christian's face was pale and his eyes had difficulty staying open. He needed some place to rest and soon. Hopeful was scared. *King, help us.*

"Whoa! Hey, Chris! Check out this place!" Hopeful came to a sudden halt, forcing Christian to stop.

"What, bro?"

Christian looked up, following Hopeful's gaze down the path. Just beyond them, the King's Path widened into a grassy meadow with tall welcoming sugar maple and overladen fruit trees. From where they stood, they could hear running water. "Let's go, man! We can rest there!" Hopeful began to pull Christian along, impatiently.

"Hold up! I'll get there," Christian replied irritated, yanking his arm away from Hopeful. Inwardly though, he was thankful that the King provided a place for him to rest. *You came through again, King. Thanks.*

As the two got closer, they noticed a large portion of the green meadow was enclosed by a solid stone fence. As Hopeful unfastened the gate latch, he exclaimed, "Man, look at this place!" It was such a beautiful restful place! Flowers of every color in the rainbow grew in the soft green grass. Birds lifted their beaks in melodic melodies as if singing a love song to their Creator. Christian spotted a waterfall cascading over rocks, spilling into a river that meandered its way lazily through the meadow. Ripe pears, apples, and peaches hung abundantly from branches and the leaves of the sugar maple trees welcomed weary pilgrims into their cool shade.

After biting into the juicy sweetness of a pear, Christian sat down in the plush grass thick as carpet, resting against its tree trunk that seemed to conform to his back perfectly. He closed his eyes. Everything was so still and peaceful here! The boys ate the delicious fruit and Christian loosened his armor. He soon fell asleep, resting on the plush green grass.

As soon as Christian woke up from his much-needed nap, the boys heard a friendly voice, seeming to come out of nowhere.

"HE—LL—OO! Hey there, pilgrims!" Christian and Hopeful looked in the direction of the voice and saw a man waving, coming toward them from the far end of the meadow.

"Evangelist?" Christian squinted in the distance. "Is that Evangelist?!"

"Evangelist? You mean the guy who showed me the way to the King's Path? That Evangelist?"

"Yeah. That Evangelist." As the man came closer, Christian noticed that it was his friend wearing his trademark dark suit.

The boys waved as he approached, carrying a picnic basket in one hand and a bag in the other hand. With a wide smile, he greeted the boys, extending his hand. "Hello, Christian and Hopeful! It is so good to see you boys again!"

"Good to see you too." Christian always liked meeting Evangelist, although he hoped this time Evangelist didn't have another warning for him. He didn't have the strength nor the will to go through something like the Haunted Valley or Vanity Fair again.

With his arms outstretched, Evangelist asked the boys, "So, what do you guys think of this place?"

"This place is amazing!" Hopeful didn't even wait to answer, and lifted his half-eaten apple. "And the food is um, um good!" Christian nodded his head in agreement.

Evangelist smiled and glanced at Christian, with a wink. "It's much different than the Haunted Valley or Vanity Fair, isn't it?" Then catching the concerned look in Christian's eyes and as if reading his thoughts, he quickly added, "Don't worry. I'm not here with a warning this time." His deep throaty chuckle filled the air and Christian found himself laughing along. No matter what the situation, Evangelist always had a way of making people feel at ease like everything was going to be okay.

"Mind if I sit with you boys for a bit?" Before waiting for the answer, Evangelist plopped himself down on the plush grass, placing the basket and bag next to him, and let out a big sigh. "The King sent me to tell you that He would like you to stay here for a couple of days. This place is called the Valley of Peace. Pretty incredible place. Made by the King Himself for His pilgrims. The Wicked Prince or any of his minions cannot come within these walls, so there's nothing to fear here. No sir! Nothing to fear."

Nodding at Christian, he continued, "I see you even loosened up your armor a bit. Good for you!" He slapped Christian on his arm. "You won't need it here! No sir!"

Christian winced at the friendly slap and Evangelist's face grew serious. "I saw what happened in Vanity Fair. Sorry to hear about Faithful, although we all know she's in a better place. I'm real proud of you, Christian, for keeping your focus on the King. But that Allure sure is a looker, isn't she?"

Christian nodded. "Yeah. She is."

Hopeful added, "There's lots of good lookin' chicks in Vanity Fair. But . . ."

Evangelist cast a fatherly look at him. "But what, Son?"

Hopeful looked downward. Although he knew he was forgiven, he still felt the sting of guilt and shame. "But I found out the hard way that there's so much more to life than parties and hot chicks."

Evangelist leaned back and let out a loud belly laugh. "A good lesson learned, my Son. There's nothin' wrong with lookin'; just don't buy before it's your time! The King has somebody picked out for each of you—one that not only looks good on the outside, but is beautiful on the inside and loves Him too. Trust the King and wait until He brings her to you." Turning to Christian, he asked sincerely, "How are you feeling?"

"Better than I was, but still very sore. Still haven't gotten my energy back yet."

"Well, this place is perfect for your health and restoration, Chris! See that river over there? That is the River of Life. Yes sir! Its name says it all! Its cool waters will not only quench your thirst, but will refresh and restore your health. Drink that water and you'll feel better in no time, Chris!"

"Do you have a cup in that basket, Evangelist? I could get some water for Christian." Christian smiled at his friend's helpfulness. *He should've been called Helpful.*

"Well, well! Thanks, Hopeful! I almost forgot about the basket." Evangelist opened its lid and peered into it, lifting out two cups and giving them to Hopeful. "The King packed this Himself and sent it to you. Wanted you to have a nice dinner. Hmmm . . . let's see here. Looks like He really knows you two boys!" Taking the containers out of the basket, the boys yelled in unison, "Nachos and pizza!" "Yes!!!"

As Hopeful ran off to the River of Life, Evangelist took advantage of the opportunity to ask Christian about his adventures since the last time they met. And as always, Christian enjoyed the conversation and felt encouraged by Evangelist's presence and wisdom.

"You gotta check out this water, man!" Hopeful came back with the cups full, his face beaming. "Man, Evangelist! You weren't kidding—this water is off the chain!"

Christian smiled as he gratefully accepted a cup of the revitalizing liquid. As he swallowed, he could feel the cool life-giving water flowing through his aching body, restoring his energy and health. *This is good stuff. Thanks, King!*

Evangelist looked at his watch. "Oh, my! Gotta get back. Lost track of time!" Standing up, he told the boys, "Oh, I almost forgot. Over yonder through the meadow is a log cabin where you boys can sleep and shower—indoor plumbing and all! It's quite comfortable with all the comforts of home."

Picking up the bag, Evangelist turned to the boys and winked. "Oh, and the King wanted you two to have this." He reached in, and pulled out...

"A football!" Both boys cried out in unison, as Evangelist tossed it to Hopeful. "Thanks, King!"

"See you boys later! Remember, keep following the King's Path!" And with a wave, Evangelist walked away.

Hopeful turned to Christian. "Wanna eat first or play catch?"

26
CAUGHT UP!

"**1, 2, 3** . . . Hut!" Hopeful backed up a few steps and threw a perfect spiral to Christian's waiting arms. Christian ran it in the makeshift end zone for a touchdown. "Boo-yah!"

It was just like ol' times, except this place was close to paradise, which was a far cry from D'City. The week flew by quickly as the boys played catch, relaxed, ate delicious satisfying fruit, and slept. Christian's energy and strength returned and his wounds healed so that he felt like his normal self again.

"Good throw, H!" Christian jogged over to him for a high-five.

"Ready to get goin', Chris? It's still early; we can get a good ways in the daylight."

"Yeah, I know. Guess we can't stay here forever. Sure, let's go."

Together, they gathered up their few belongings and picked some fruit to take with them on their journey. After Christian fastened his armor and put his helmet on, he picked up his trusty sword and shield. "Gotta be prepared. You never know what lies ahead!"

Hopeful slapped him on his back. "Let's go, man! The Celestial City awaits!"

The boys were feeling good as they once again headed down the King's Path. Time flew by quickly as the boys occupied themselves with playing catch and roastin' each other good-naturedly. Suddenly, Christian stopped, pointing to the path before them. "Look, bro!" The King's Path appeared to be a dead end into a large field, making it difficult to tell where it continued.

"That's strange. What should we do?" Hopeful was convinced that Christian knew more about the King and His ways than he did.

Christian glanced around at their surroundings before answering. Not seeing any other good alternatives, he answered, "Well, Evangelist said the King's Path is almost always straight. So, I think we should just keep going straight and see what happens."

"Okay. Then let's go!" Together, Hopeful and Christian walked on through the field, confident in their choice. Before long, though, the grass became desert-like with rough stones and hard ground. Walking became increasingly difficult and confidence surrendered to confusion and doubt.

"You sure this is the way, Chris? I don't have boots like yours. My ankles are turnin' somethin' bad on these darn stones, man. I can't keep goin' on like this, man. This is crazy!"

Confusion clouded Christian's face. "I don't know, bro. I thought for sure this was the way. This place just doesn't make sense, though. Walking on this stuff sure zaps my energy."

Exasperated, Hopeful looked at his friend and sighed. "So now what?"

Christian took an apple out of his pocket and bit into its juiciness, as if doing so would give him answers. He was so concentrated on their predicament and solving it himself, that he didn't even think of asking the King or reading the Book for answers. After a few more bites, Christian spoke his thoughts. "Maybe I was wrong, bro, and this isn't the way. It just doesn't feel right now. It's just so unclear. The King's Path should be obvious, right?"

"You askin' me, man?" Hopeful seemed surprised. "Well…I've been noticin' that meadow over there." He pointed to the left and Christian gazed in that direction. *Why didn't we see that before?* Hopeful continued, "The low fence that borders it looks like it runs parallel to this wilderness. We could just hop the fence and…"

"…We could just hop back over if we had to." Christian finished Hopeful's thought. He didn't have any better ideas, so he agreed. "Let's go and check it out!"

As they approached the fence, Christian exclaimed, "That meadow almost looks like the Valley of Peace where we just came from. Good lookin' out, H!"

Without hesitating, Hopeful vaulted over the waist-high fence. "Man, it's nice over here. The ground is nice and smooth and there's a clear marked path! C'mon, Chris!"

Just as Christian was getting ready to follow Hopeful's lead, a flicker of doubt flashed in his mind. *You really sure about this, Chris? Remember the last "shortcut" you took? The last path?*

"You comin', man?"

"You sure 'bout this, H?" Christian voiced his sudden doubt.

"Why you doubtin' all of a sudden? Sure looks safe and smooth. Besides, like we said, we can hop back over whenever we want to."

And without a second thought, Christian hopped over the fence to join his friend. All doubts were quickly erased when he discovered that this new path was much easier to walk on. Before long, they came upon a curly-haired boy sitting alone at the side of the path. He was so absorbed in playing his video game that he didn't even notice the two boys approach.

Christian spoke first. "Hi there!"

The boy mumbled "Hey!" without even looking up. His thumbs were moving at rapid speeds as he tried to fight his enemies onscreen.

Hopeful tried to get the boy's attention. "Excuse me. Don't mean to bother you, but could you tell us where this path goes?"

"To the Celestial City." The boy continued to be transfixed on his game.

Hopeful elbowed Christian. "See! I told you! We have nothin' to worry about!"

Christian and Hopeful could see that the boy did not want to be bothered, so they thanked him and continued on their way, laughing and talking and enjoying the newfound ease of the journey.

Later that afternoon, the sky suddenly became eerily dark. Hopeful declared, "Looks like a storm's comin'. We should probably try to find shelter. This one looks big."

Christian looked up and agreed. "Yeah, that's a good idea." No sooner were the words out of his mouth when heavy raindrops pelted them and lightning flashes tore jagged edges into the sky.

"Let's run toward the fence! We'll be okay!" Hopeful yelled into the storm, hoping Christian could hear him over the roaring thunder. Running in the supposed direction of the fence, both boys quickly became disoriented.

"The fence should've been here, man! Can't see it anywhere!" Christian screamed to be heard.

"I don't get this! Hey, over here!" Lightning had illuminated a small red tent almost hidden in the bushes and Hopeful had spotted it. Drenched to the bone, the two boys crawled inside thankful for this temporary shelter. Christian tried to zip the door shut, but the zipper stuck fast. No matter how hard he or Hopeful tried, they couldn't get it to close in the darkness. "Oh, man!"

"Don't worry. The rain's not coming in, so we'll be okay. We'll just wait this storm out." Hopeful's words did little to encourage Christian. He knew in his gut that this was not the right way. Shame and guilt washed over him. *How could I have been so stupid again? I should've said something to Hopeful. I knew better.* He had let struggle get the best of him. He was thankful that Hopeful could not see the tears streaking down his face. The pitch blackness and torrential storm surrounding them reflected the deep gloominess in his soul.

"Hopeful, I'm . . ." Christian could barely get the words out. He took a breath and tried again, louder so Hopeful could hear him above the raindrops that the tent's nylon fabric seemed to magnify. "I'm so sorry that I got us in this mess."

Hopeful put his hand on Christian's shoulder. "It was both of us, man. We'll be okay."

But Christian was not convinced. *How many chances will the King give me?* Both boys huddled together in the cramped space, shivering with cold and fright, hoping the storm would end and morning would come soon.

After a sleepless night and weak from exhaustion, hunger, and uncertainty, Christian and Hopeful welcomed the dim daylight. The storm was over. Stretching their muscles, the boys were anxious to get out of the too-small tent and get back to the King's Path. "Looks like it's goin' be a cloudy day today, bro," Christian declared as he peeked out the tent's opening. Suddenly, a giant black menacing shadow appeared. Both Hopeful and Christian looked at each other wide-eyed, paralyzed with fear. *What/who was making that shadow?*

A deep gruff voice boomed in mock surprise, "Well, well, well. What have we here?" Giant Despair, one of the most famous soldiers in the Wicked Prince's army, was out for a walk to see if there was any storm damage on his property. As he was walking, the gleam off of Christian's helmet caught his eye. He reached in the tent and in a single swoop, seized both boys in his giant-sized fist.

Holding them close to his face, he exclaimed with his eyes bulging, "Armor? Are you for real pilgrims?!! Well, well! It must be my lucky day!" His foul breath reeked of rotten fish and made Christian gag. Hopeful caught a glimpse of gold-capped teeth amongst rotten cavities in the giant's mouth. Both boys dared not say a word, thankful at least they were together in this nightmare.

Their captor stood well over nine feet tall with a layer of fat covering his stocky muscular body, and was dressed in a dirty ripped T-shirt and brown cotton slacks. A full unkempt afro and nappy beard framed his ugly, scarred face, accented with a jagged scar on his left cheek. "Now you are in my power! You belong to me!!" He let out a malicious laugh that sent shivers up and down the already-chilled pilgrims. Stuffing them in a bag that smelled of human waste, vomit, and decay, he shouted triumphantly, "Gotcha, suckas!" Shivering from dampness and sheer terror, the boys could scarcely breathe in this disgusting enclosed prison.

The giant brought his prisoners to his home, Doubting Castle. Opening the door, he shouted to his wife, "Honey, I'm home! Come! I have somethin' to show you!"

The boys heard footsteps shuffle into the room and a lady's crackled voice answer. "What is it, dear?"

The giant opened the bag and dumped the boys onto a large splintered wooden table, laughing with evil delight. His wife, whose name was Insecurity, clapped her chubby hands in happiness and smiled a toothless grin.

"Pilgrims?! Good for you! Where did you find them?" She bent down toward them and poked at them with a crooked arthritic finger. "Look at these stupid creatures! Are they even alive?" The boys were scared stiff and couldn't move a muscle.

"What should I do with them, honey? Can't leave them on our kitchen table!" The giant roared, as if he just told the funniest joke.

Insecurity answered quickly, "They are worthless crea-tures. Lock them in the dungeon. But, beat them first so they learn a lesson not to intrude where they don't belong. Those stupid good-for-nothin' fools." Clucking her tongue, she shuffled away to stir a green vile-smelling stew that was boil-ing in a large black pot.

Huddled together for warmth and companionship, Chris-tian and Hopeful lay miserably on the stone-cold dungeon concrete floor, damp and sore. The threadbare scratchy wool blankets they were given did not offer much needed warmth, as they were full of holes. They heard the thick wooden door slam shut and lock and knew there was no escape. With no food or water, they drifted in and out of consciousness, quickly losing track of time.

"I wonder what's going to happen to us," Christian eventu-ally whispered to Hopeful, his throat parched and scratching. Rats scurried about them with ease, having the freedom of going in and out of the prison cell. *I never thought rodents would have a better life than me.* His heart was especially heavy with sorrow and guilt for getting them both in this pre-dicament and the voices were back running continuously in his mind. *I should've known better. I'm so stupid. I'm never going to make it to the Celestial City. Maybe I was never meant to go there after all. This is what I deserve. The King's not going to keep giving me chance after chance. I blew it big this time.*

Christian was momentarily distracted from the irritating depressing voices by the creak of the dungeon door opening. Turning their heads, both Hopeful and Christian saw Insecurity's recognizable hand shove a bowl of the steaming green goop into their cell. "Dinner is served, you brainless monkeys! Enjoy!" And with a merciless cackle, she slammed the door behind her. Click. The lock turned, audibly mocking any dreams of escape.

With every ounce of energy, Hopeful crawled over to the awful smelling liquid. "Ewwww! What is this?"

Christian propped his head on his hand, his elbow resting on the cold, unyielding floor. "Probably poison. Smells like somethin' died in it."

"Well, we gotta eat somethin, Chris. If not, we'll starve to death."

"Face it, H. There's no way we're gettin' out of here. Might as well either eat it and take our chances or you're right. We'll die a slow death of starvation."

27

ESCAPE

old up, Chris. There's always hope. Let's think."
Together, the boys fought against hunger, pain, and sleeplessness as they brainstormed ways of survival and escape. Catching and eating mice was unthinkable. The small window near the ceiling was too narrow and high up to reach. Christian didn't have the strength to wield his sword or shield, and besides they were puny compared to the giant's huge weapons. Every idea they came up with was either impossible or unrealistic.

Defeat washed over Christian. "See, H? Like I told you, we're good as dead here." The crippling voices started up again in Christian's mind, louder this time.

But Hopeful didn't listen to Christian. *There has to be a way! There's always a way! What are we missing?*

Just then, the dungeon door opened and a giant-sized shadow filled the room. Surprised to see the boys still alive and the stew untouched, Giant Despair was filled with a jealous rage. "You stupid dogs! Who do you think you are? You waitin' for your supposed King? He won't show up—ever! You are as good as dead. I should beat you for bein' so stupid." And with that, he raised his immense club, his eyes bulging and skin soaked with rancid sweat.

"Please, stop! Have mercy on us!" Hopeful begged.

Giant Despair hesitated mid-swing and snarled. "What, you fool? You want mercy? I'll give you mercy!" And with a roar, he lunged at Hopeful.

Hopeful cringed back, his arms shielding his face from the impending blow. Suddenly without warning, a bright light streamed through the window slit, filling the entire dungeon cell with dazzling brilliance.

"AAAAAGH! NOOOOO!"

Almost as if by magic, the club dropped from the giant's deathly grip, hitting the floor with a thud. Giant Despair screamed in rage and pain, temporarily blinded and weak. Insecurity heard his agonizing screams and shuffled to him as fast as her over-sized body would allow, which took several minutes. "Oh, dear. Not again." She pulled him along out of the dungeon and shut the door. Click.

When they had gone, Christian looked at Hopeful with shock and bewilderment. "What just happened?"

Hopeful let out a nervous relieved snicker. There was no way he would have survived that beat down. He seemed as shocked as Christian was. "It had somethin' to do with the light, I think. Man, that was tripped out!" He paused, his face beaming with a new revelation. "That's it! Duh! That's what we've been missin'—the King!"

Christian stared at Hopeful, as the voice in his head screamed. *See how stupid you are forgetting about the King?*

*You were never good enough and never will be. You're hope-
less!*

The boys had been so focused on their problems and pain,
they had completely forgotten about the One who had the
answers they so desperately needed.

"Let's pray to the King for help." Christian nodded and
Hopeful began, "King, we are sorry for our wrong choice of
leaving Your path and then forgetting about You. Please forgive us. You have been so good to us in the past and we know
that You have the power and strength to help us now in this
overwhelmingly hopeless prison. Show us how to get back
to You. In Your great and mighty Name," and Christian said in
unison, "Amen!"

No sooner was "Amen" spoken when Christian felt a heavy
coolness press against his chest. It was a strange sensation,
but unmistakable. Instinctively, he put his hand on the spot
and gasped. With a sudden burst of energy, he yelled, "Hopeful! I got it! The Key of Promise! I totally forgot!"

Hopeful looked at Christian quizzically. "What?"

"No, I got it! I had it the whole time! Our way of escape!
Man, I can't believe I forgot all about it!" Christian paused to
catch his breath. "The Key of Promise! Truth and Discretion
gave it to me as I was leaving the Palace Beautiful." He remembered her words like she said them yesterday. He didn't
understand them then, but he understood them now. "She

said, 'May it unlock doors that imprison you in darkness and bring you back into the light.'" Christian held up the golden key and recited one of the King's promises. "The King will supply all of our needs according to the riches of His glory."[1]

"Wow!" Hopeful's eyes were wide. "That's so cool, man! The King came through again for us." He thought for a second and continued, "So, when and how are we going to use it to escape?"

Before Christian could answer, they heard heavy footsteps deliberately coming toward them and an evil menacing voice roared, "If you are still alive, you two stupid dogs, get ready for the beat down of your life! I'll show you who is the most powerful!" The dungeon door opened and there Giant Despair stood, staring at them in complete disbelief that they were still alive, let alone standing up! No other pilgrims ever survived this long. Rage flooded his entire body and with an out-of-control crazed mind, he lunged at the two boys, his club raised high. "I'm going to kill you both!" Just then, glorious bright light streamed through the window, as if it were a heavenly blanket of protection over the pilgrims.

"AAAAAAAGH!"

The giant was once again overcome by blindness, his muscles weakened like a newborn baby's. Dropping the club, he screamed, "Wait 'til I get my sight back! I'm goin' to deep fry

The giant was overcome by blindness.

you, you jive turkeys!" And with that, he ran out of the cell in agony forgetting to close the door behind him.

"Now!"

Christian and Hopeful saw their chance to escape from their foul-smelling evil kidnapper. They ran out of the dungeon cell, energized by an unseen Power. They had no idea how to navigate their way through the castle, but were confident that their King would make a way.

"Let's just follow Him. Keep your eyes open for a way out," Christian whispered. The two boys followed at a safe distance, watchin' each other's back to make sure that Mrs. Giant wasn't around.

"Over there!" Hopeful pointed to the kitchen door and whispered, "I see light comin' through the bottom. That's the way out. I'm sure of it!" Making their way over to the door, to the boys' dismay, they found the doorknob was out of reach—way above their heads.

"Bummer! What do we do now?" Hopeful scratched his head, puzzled.

"Let's push a chair over. I'll climb up, put the key in the lock, and bam! We'll be free! You can be on the lookout."

"Deal! Let's do it." Hopeful and Christian hurried over to the nearest chair, and with all their might, pushed it close next to the door. Christian climbed on Hopeful's shoulders and heaved himself on the seat of the chair. It reminded him of when he scrambled up trees as a little boy.

"Do you hear that? Something's in the kitchen." It was Insecurity's voice. "Go and see what it is. Better not be a gigantic rat." She shivered. "Oooo! And you know I hate rats!" The scraping of the large chair on the wooden floor as it was being moved attracted Insecurity's attention and now Giant Despair was heading toward the kitchen to investigate.

"Christian! Psst! The big dude is coming!"

Christian's hand froze in place. "For real?" He almost had the key in the lock.

Just then, Giant Despair stormed into the kitchen, stunned to see the two pilgrims as the "rat." Surprise gave way quickly to fury. "I said you two will not escape! And I meant it! You will die!!" Grabbing a razor-sharp cleaver from the knife block, he rushed at the two. The boys froze in sheer terror, only two words escaping their lips in unison.

"King, help!"

Immediately, a dazzling heavenly light penetrated through the kitchen window's blinds, causing the predictable painful reaction for Giant Despair. The cleaver dropped from his grasp and plummeted directly on the giant's toes of his right foot, chopping them clean off.

"OOOOOWWWWW!!!!" Howling in double agony, the giant crumpled to the floor, grasping his mangled bleeding foot.

"Now!" Christian raised his arm confidently, inserting the key into the lock. It fit perfectly. Click.

"Yes!" Hopeful pumped his fist in excitement and victory. The door swung open as if by magic. Christian jumped down from the chair, and sprung into a forward roll to protect his landing. "Go!"

Together, they ran as fast as they could, propelled by adrenaline and an invisible source of energy and strength. Over the threshold and down the overgrown thorny path, they ran and didn't dare look back. The cool invigorating fresh air stung their lungs, and the bright daylight burned their eyes, but freedom never felt so good. Doubting Castle was behind them forever.

"The fence!" Christian spotted the welcomed destination first and pointed. He smiled mischievously at Hopeful. "I'll race ya! And the last one is a jive turkey!"

....

[1] Philippians 4:19 NIV

28
IGNORANCE

"Dude! That was close! I thought we were goners for sure." Christian could barely speak. He was relieved to be free, but all the time in the dungeon was taking its toll. Now that the two were back on the King's Path, the need to find food became their first priority. They began to walk and, almost immediately, came to a small grassy oasis in the middle of the desert-like field. There the boys found some juicy delicious fruit and cool water from the River of Life, pumped from a well built by the King Himself.

"Man, I'll never take another easy shortcut again," Hopeful said as he took another refreshing drink.

"Yeah, you'd think I would've learned somethin' from the first time I took a shortcut. That didn't end so well either. If it wasn't for the King, my journey would've ended before I had even reached the Shepherd's Gate."

All of a sudden, Hopeful's face grew serious, full of concern. "I think we need to warn other pilgrims about those monsters. Maybe we can keep someone from making the same stupid choice we did."

"How do you think we should do that?"

Hopeful thought for a minute. "I think we should make a sign. You could use your sword to carve words into a rock."

"Good idea! Now we just have to find a rock big enough."

Together, the two backtracked to the spot which almost caused their demise, and to their amazement, there sat a large rock just the perfect size for their task and positioned on the King's side of the fence. Taking out his sword from its sheath, Christian easily etched letters into its hard, grainy surface, as Hopeful told him what to write: "WARNING! This property belongs to Giant Despair, a servant of the Wicked Prince. DO NOT ENTER or you will die!"

Satisfied with the thought of helping other pilgrims who may be tempted, Christian put his sword in his sheath and he and Hopeful continued on down the King's Path. The rough stony pebbles didn't seem so troublesome and painful now. Eventually, the path became smooth again as it continued through a patch of evergreen trees.

"Hi there!"

Christian and Hopeful jumped at the unexpected voice. "Oh, hey!"

To their left, a slender caramel-haired pale-skinned boy stood at the edge of a narrow crooked path that intersected the King's Path. Noticing Christian's armor, he asked, "Are you two going to the Celestial City?"

"Yes we are!" Christian answered. "And you?"

"Of course!" replied the boy confidently.

Trying to be friendly to the stranger, Hopeful introduced them both. "I'm Hopeful and this is Christian."

"Nice to meet you both. I'm Ignorance."

"Where did you come from?" Christian asked suspiciously, since the path the boy emerged from looked strange.

Ignorance stuck out his chest and stood up taller. "Why, the city of Pride, of course!"

Walking all together down the path, Hopeful glanced sideways at Christian. Neither of them had heard of that place before. Christian sized the boy up, and smiled to himself. Back in D'City, people would call Ignorance a "nerd" with his bright orange-rimmed oversized glasses, his hair parted to the side, and his navy blue vest worn over a periwinkle button-down shirt paired with jeans. This dude was definitely a yuppie.

Christian seemed somewhat confused and asked Ignorance, "Hey, man. Where's your scroll?"

"Scroll? What scroll? Why do I need a stupid scroll?"

"Everyone needs a scroll to enter the Celestial City."

"I don't need that. Why everyone knows that everybody who does good gets in! Besides, the King loves everybody so He won't turn anyone away. Duh!"

Hopeful joined the conversation. "Yes, it's true that the King does love everybody and wants everyone to be with Him in the Celestial City, but He does ask that we have a scroll to show at the gates of the Celestial City."

With eyes narrowed and distrust in his voice, Ignorance questioned, "How do you know? Why do you think your view is right?"

Christian took the Book out of his cargo pants pocket. "This Book, written by the King Himself, says so."

"Yeah," Hopeful continued, backing Christian up. "You have to enter through the Shepherd's Gate and pass by the Cross. There you are given the life-giving scroll."

Ignorance dismissed the Book with a wave of his hand. "Hogwash! That Book was written by men, not the King! As for the Gate and Cross, it was probably easy for you to get to them. For me, they are too far from where I live. Besides, the people from my city just take that path over there when they want to get to the King. It ends up in the same place and is much quicker and easier. All paths eventually lead to the King."

His forehead wrinkling, Christian forced himself to remember how Gramps or Evangelist would answer that. *Oh, yeah! That's it!* He spoke aloud, "The King's Son said that He was the only way and the truth and the life and that no one comes to the King except through Him."[1]

Ignorance laughed. "Ha! That's ridiculous! I've never heard of such nonsense! Good people go to the Celestial City and I know I'm a good person. I don't swear, cheat, or lie. I'm nice to everybody, work hard, and go to church." He paused. "Well, most of the time. I also know all about the King's Son. Look, I don't feel like talking to you guys anymore. You both go on to the Celestial City your way and I'll get there my way.

Life is better when I live it my way." And with that, Ignorance bounded on ahead of them.

Hopeful glanced at Christian. "What was that about?"

"I dunno. That dude's a knucklehead. Let's just keep goin'."

Hopeful shrugged his shoulders. "We gotta be gettin' close to the Celestial City, don't you think?"

Christian's mind was still on Ignorance. "Man, I wonder what will happen to Knucklehead when he gets to the Gates without the scroll."

"He made his choice."

Christian covered his scroll with his hand protectively. "At least we don't have to worry about that. We have our scrolls."

"Yeah. I'm glad we paid attention and chose to follow the true King's Path."

....

[1] John 14:6 NIV

29
TOO LATE!

The King's Path was now narrower than it had ever been. The boys followed it carefully until it came to an end underneath a narrow archway with intricate carvings similar to the ones found on the boys' scroll containers. After walking through the archway, Christian and Hopeful stood at the base of a stone stairway carved into the side of a mountain. Maple tree boughs shaded the stairway, as if bowing down to the pilgrims travelling its steps.

"I wonder what these carvings say," Hopeful wondered aloud.

"Don't know. Gotta know the King's ancient language to be able to read it. C'mon! Let's start climbin'. Looks like we have a ways to go." With Christian leading the way up, the boys were fascinated by many different statues perched on the stair walls. Some of them were cherubim-like creatures and others resembled the Shining Ones. Their wings stretched over the path, creating a protective archway. After a somewhat lengthy climb, Christian and Hopeful counted to three and hopped the last step together.

"Look!" The path before them became a road of golden bricks running between multiple rows of cozy cottages on either side. The people here were dressed in robes of beige and white, just like the people wore in the days when the Book was written.

Hopeful turned to Christian. "Dude, is this place for real?"

Before Christian could answer, a woman approached them, smiling warmly. "Hello, there! Welcome to the city of Zion! We are so glad you are here. My name is Friendly."

"I'm Christian and this is Hopeful." A puzzled expression came over his face. "Zion? You mean this isn't the Celestial City?"

"Heavens, no! This place? The Celestial City is more beautiful and unlike any place you've ever seen. At least, that's what I've been told, not that I've seen it yet. But you two have made it this far and the King is pleased with you. Here you will stay until the King calls for you. Only when He calls for you, may you see the Celestial City and go into His presence. He keeps a thick mist in front of the City so we can't even catch a glimpse of it before our time. Come, and I'll introduce you to some friends of mine and show you where you will stay."

Christian and Hopeful followed the woman through the village streets baffled by the welcoming attitudes of the people they passed by. Neither one of the boys could remember a time in D'City when they ever had to say "hello" or "good morning" so many times in their entire life! Friendly led them to an area of the city that opened to a large park with a beautiful centralized marble fountain, picnic tables, and benches. Hopeful leaned toward Christian and whispered, "Kind of looks like Destruction Park, but better, right?" Christian smiled and nodded, thankful those days were behind him.

Friendly walked over to a small group of people sitting at a picnic table, laughing as they played a card game. Clapping her hands to get their attention, she excitedly exclaimed, "Hey everybody! We have some more family members!" For the next few minutes, Christian and Hopeful were lovingly welcomed by these strangers like two long-distant cousins attending their first family reunion. "Come join us! There's room at the table for two more!"

"Maybe later," Friendly answered. "Right now, I have to get these two settled in to where they'll be staying." Pointing to a brick cottage across the street from the park, she said, "Do you see the house there with the blue shutters? That is the house the King has provided for both of you to stay at until your time has come to cross over. Everything you need is already there for you."

"Do you know when He'll be calling us and what we have to do to cross over?" Hopeful asked, curiously.

An elderly man, whose name was Jovial, chuckled. "You boys are excited and inquisitive. I like those qualities in young men. I remember when I was as young as you two." He laughed as if the memory delighted him. "Only the King knows when your days here with us are over. He will call you when it is the right time. When He calls you, you shall have to cross the Dark River before getting to the gates of the Celestial City with your scroll in hand. Yes, sir. You shall have to jump in those murky waters all by yourself as the last act of trust in the King's help."

Hopeful and Christian both glanced at each other, as if they were thinking the same thing. *What about Ignorance? What's going to happen to him?* Although they barely knew him, they couldn't help but feel somewhat responsible, and yet, curious about his fate.

Christian couldn't contain himself and spoke to the group, "Hey! Have any of you seen a guy with four eyes, I mean, really thick glasses, named Ignorance?"

The card-playing group nodded their heads, as if he were hard to forget. Jovial spoke. "Yes, he was here. He is like so many others who have taken shortcuts and who have done all the right things for all the wrong reasons. They believe themselves to be good righteous people, but in the eyes of the King, their hearts are not in the right place. We tried to talk him out of going farther and gave him direction on the way he should go, but he refused to listen. He wanted to be left alone. We are not permitted to stop anyone who has made it this far, so we let him leave. His fate is now in the hands of the King."

"How long ago was this?" Christian asked.

"Oh, he left just moments before you two arrived."

"We have to try one last time to stop him," Christian exclaimed enthusiastically. "C'mon! Let's go!"

So the boys got up and ran in the direction that Jovial said he went, hoping to catch him.

"Wait you two! You mustn't leave before . . . Oh dear!" Friendly's voice was soft and full of concern for the two young men who ran away recklessly in search of their friend. "What will become of them?"

"Their fate also rests in the hands of the King. We shall pray for their safe return," said Jovial.

"IGNORANCE! YO, IGNORANCE!" The boys cupped their hands to their mouths, screaming in all directions as they ran, hoping to get his attention. Receiving no answer, they continued to run, quickly finding themselves in a forest that seemed to be closing in around them. Hopeful put his hand on Christian's chest, stopping them. "Hey, man! Is it me or is the sky disappearing?"

Christian took a moment to look up and saw nothing but tree leaves and branches all around. "No, it's not just you. I can't see anything but trees either."

"Maybe we weren't supposed to come after Ignorance after all," Hopeful said uncertainly.

"Don't be silly, H. The King would never stop a pilgrim from saving another pilgrim. Would He?"

"I don't know right now, man. All I know is we're lost."

"No, we're not. All we have to do is turn around and go back the way we came. We should be out of the forest in no time." Christian sounded like the hopeful one this time.

"Okay, smarty pants. You lead the way."

Christian turned around in the direction he believed they came from. But after walking aimlessly through the trees which seemed to be getting closer and closer together, he admittedly stopped and said, "Dude, I think we're lost for real."

"So what do we do now?" Hopeful was exasperated and out of answers.

Christian admitted, "This is my fault entirely. I was the one who wanted to find Ignorance. I was the one who wanted to save somebody. But I guess it's not for me to save anybody. Guess all we can do is point a person to the Truth. They must open their hearts and the King will do the rest. Since it was my idea to foolishly run after Ignorance, I will pray to the King for your deliverance and any punishment of this wrong choice should be taken out on me only." Christian kneeled and folded his hands and began to talk earnestly to the King. But before he could utter five syllables, he heard a voice that was kind, true, and full of authority, calling his name.

"Christian."

He began to look around.

"Hey, hey! Do you hear that?"

"Hear what?" Hopeful asked.

"Christian." The voice spoke again.

"There it goes again. Hey, you sure you don't hear that?" Christian asked disbelievingly.

Hopeful looked at Christian, worried. "Dude, you okay?"

"Follow My voice, my son, and I will lead you out of here."

Christian grabbed Hopeful and began to walk in the direction he believed the voice to be coming from. "C'mon! Just follow me."

"It was honorable for you to want to save Ignorance. But, a cup that is already full cannot receive the water of life. He has chosen his own path and even though you foolishly ran into My forest before it was your time, I know that you did it out of love and concern. And for this reason alone, I will grant you passage."

Suddenly, the trees began to clear and a light so bright shone down, hurting the boys' eyes. The sound of rushing water could be heard all around them. Christian and Hopeful cautiously pushed their way through a cluster of bushes.

"Whoa, buddy." Hopeful's arm raised just in time to stop Christian from going over a cliff.

"Whoa! Thanks, H! That is a long way down." Fifty feet below where they were standing was a river of rushing water so dark and green that it almost appeared black.

"Man, I'm not ever jumpin' in there!" declared Christian. "Do you think that is the river the old guy was talking about?"

"Sure looks like a Dark River to me. I don't think that's a question that needs answerin.' I'm startin' to think you hung around Ignorance too long." Hopeful punched him in the shoulder, playfully.

"Whatever, man. Speaking of Knucklehead, look! There he is!" Hopeful's gaze followed Christian's pointed finger.

"What? He found a boat? Who is that rowing it?"

Only a few feet from the riverbank closest to the boys, Ignorance could be seen lying comfortably in the back of a lavishly decorated boat that reminded the boys of the ones used in Venice. But the guy piloting the boat definitely was not from Venice! He wore a robe of deep shiny black material with an oversized hood that covered most of his face, exposing only his very large and sharp teeth. The sight of his teeth made Christian shudder, reminding him of the Wicked Prince.

The boys watched quietly, in awe and anxious anticipation, as the boat docked on the opposite side of the river. Once there, Ignorance could be seen almost skipping toward a very large Shining One dressed in golden armor, standing close to the City Gates. Even though Christian and Hopeful could not hear what was being said, they could tell by their body language what was going on.

The Shining One wanted to see Ignorance's scroll and stood with arms folded across his chest, waiting patiently as Ignorance pretended to be looking for that which he never had. After a moment, Ignorance appeared to be pleading as he had so many times before, but to no avail. Then, just as before, Christian could hear a voice booming loudly, "Depart from Me. I never knew you!"[1]

The Shining One wanted
to see Ignorance's scroll.

Christian knew the voice belonged to the King and that Ignorance would not enter the Celestial City. The Shining One raised his muscular arm, pointing toward the dark figure lurking patiently by the boat. The creature smiled hungrily at his weak and helpless prey. His large pointy fangs glowed from the reflection of an eerie blue light oozing its way toward Ignorance. The light, having a life of its own, surrounded the now horrified Ignorance as the reality of his choice finally set in. It was too late. Wrapping him up and lifting him in the air, the light illuminated the ground beneath him which opened to reveal a fiery pit. Ignorance's terror-stricken pleas for help could be heard clearly by the boys until the earth closed up and swallowed him whole.

There was a moment of silence before the figure released a sinister bone-chilling laugh. *I knew it! He was a Prince's minion.* Christian shuddered again.

"SILENCE! Be gone from here, Demon! You have found no victory here. That which you have taken was already yours. The King has given none of those who belong to Him to you and never will! Be gone!" boomed the voice of the Shining One with power and authority.

The demon and his boat disappeared.

....

[1] Matthew 7:23

30

HOME

fter they both realized what had happened, Hopeful was the first to speak. "So, what do we do now?" Christian honestly didn't know. There was no way they could make it back on their own and he knew this to be the truth. They were lost. The only reason they made it this far was because he followed the voice of the King. After thinking for a few moments, he finally realized that they had but one choice. "I guess we have to jump."

"What? You mean down there? I thought they told us back in Zion that we have to wait to be called."

"Well, I did hear a voice that led me to this place. It was the same voice I heard telling Ignorance that He never knew him." Christian responded sounding confident.

"Hey! I heard that voice too. Maybe you're right. We couldn't have heard the voice if it wasn't meant for us to hear it, right?"

"You are correct, My sons. All that has happened was meant to happen and now I am calling you. All you need to finish your journey is to come across the river and you will have peace and rest."

Christian cautiously peered over the side of the cliff. He swallowed hard as his mind and spirit were full of conflicting thoughts and emotions. Forcing himself to look up, Christian saw the mist slowly rise, unveiling white marble walls of the city just beyond the other side of the river where peace, joy, and rest awaited him. He did trust the King. Without Him, he and his companion would never have made it this far, but the cliff stood high above the river whose dark murky waters raced toward a waterfall about 100 yards away from his anticipated point of entry. He would have little time to get his bearings and cross the river before plummeting over the edge of the waterfall.

"Hey, bro. Don't sweat this. We just gotta jump. I believe with all my heart that we'll be all right," said Hopeful.

"You're right," Christian replied. "But before I go, I better take off all this armor. I don't wanna get dragged under."

"Yeah, good idea."

As Christian began to take off his armor, he noticed the Key of Promise still around his neck. Instantly, assurances of the King filled his mind. His spirit was flooded with joy at the thought of reaching his destination and seeing his beloved Gramps again. *I'm so close, Gramps. I'm comin'. King, I know You are with me. Please help me.* Stripped of his armor and filled with newfound courage, Christian secured his scroll container over his shoulder, stepped to the side of the cliff, and dove headfirst into the scary unknown.

Fear and cold suddenly seized him as the dark waters engulfed him. Not only was he struggling to swim against the river's strong current, but the deep darkness of the water made it impossible for him to figure out which way was up.

Panic took over and his arms thrashed wildly. Christian knew he had to calm down or he would most certainly drown.

"Be still, My son, for I am with you. You are one of My flock and I have never lost one of My sheep."

Christian knew this was the voice of the Good Shepherd, the King's Son. It calmed him down enough to notice a large glowing hand reaching to rescue him from the threatening current. Grabbing on with all his might, Christian was pulled safely ashore by a mighty Shining One. Dripping wet on the riverbank, he breathed a sigh of thankfulness and smiled as he caught a glimpse of Hopeful swimming toward them with strong, confident strokes.

"Yeah, H! You can do it! Almost there!" Christian cheered his friend on toward safety.

Christian waited for his friend to come ashore and together, they eagerly handed the Guard of the Gate their scrolls. Although he wore a stern expression on his face, he unfolded his arms and accepted the containers, opening them to see if they were authentic. Meanwhile, Christian and Hopeful marveled at the sight of the white marble walls towering in front of them, surrounding this beautiful and enormous place. White marble buildings with windows of blue and purple glass, tall enough to be seen above the walls, reflected a glorious brilliance that seemed to radiate from within the city. Countless

Shining Ones flew with wings outstretched or stood guard in one of the many watchtowers on the city's walls.

"This way," the Shining One said, a welcoming smile spreading over his face, as he gestured toward the city's massive pearly gates.

Trumpets blared and a joyful chorus of "Hallelujah!" filled the air as they approached. The gates slowly swung inward, as if being opened by a great invisible hand. Christian and Hopeful gasped, their bodies tingling with a mixture of excitement and awe at their first glimpse inside the Celestial City.

"Is that my boy? Chris, is that you?"

Christian's heart stopped beating for a split second and then burst with happiness at the sight of his grandfather running toward him. He had never seen his grandfather run before and was surprised to see how fast he was.

"Gramps! Guess you really are fast!" Christian ran to Gramps and got wrapped up in a tight bear hug.

"Yes sir! Coming to the Celestial City is the best thing to happen to anyone! I'm proud and glad you made it! Living' in the Celestial City means no pain, no suffering, and no sorrow. I even got my speed back. I told you they used to call me 'The Rocket!'" Gramps winked at the boys, noticing Hopeful. "Hey, Hopeful! You made it too! Good for you!"

"I sure did! I couldn't let my buddy here trek all this way on his own. He never would have made it." Hopeful paused.

"Well, neither of us would've made it without the King's help."

"Right you are, my boy!" agreed Gramps. "Come into the presence of our King!" Putting his arms around their shoulders, he proudly walked with them. All Christian and Hopeful had seen was incredible, but it was nothing compared to the breathtaking sights that lay just behind the majestic gates.

A voice spoke from within. "I am the Alpha and the Omega—the Beginning and the End. To all who are thirsty I will give freely from the springs of the water of life. All who are victorious will inherit all these blessings, and I will be their King, and they will be my children.[1] Welcome home!"

[1] Revelation 21:6–7 NLT

DISCUSSION QUESTIONS

1. Christian followed his heart to find the Celestial City. Can you think of a time when you showed courage to follow your heart?

2. Gramps and Evangelist were older, positive influences in Christian's life who gave him wise advice to help him succeed in life. Who is the Gramps or Evangelist in your life and what was the best advice they ever gave you?

3. Several times in the story, Christian went against the popular crowd to do what he believed was right. Did you ever have to stand alone and go against being popular or liked for something that you believed was right? What happened and how did you feel?

4. Worldly Wise looked smooth and talked smooth, but tricked Christian into taking a shortcut that was harmful. Did that ever happen to you? If so, what happened and how did you escape? If not, how can you avoid being bamboozled, or tricked, like Christian?

5. The King gave Christian some great friends to help and encourage him on the long journey. Who are your best friends? How do they help you in life?

6. Each character's name in the story describes their personality. What name would you choose for you based on your personality? Why?

WORDS AND PHRASES TO KNOW AND LEARN

WORDS AND PHRASES TO KNOW AND LEARN

all-suf • fi • cient (all suh-**fish**-uhnt) *adj*
More than able to care for the needs of others

bam • boo • zle (bam-**boo**-zuhl) *verb*
To deceive, trick

blas • phe • my (**blas**-fuh-mē) *noun*
Great disrespect shown to God

ce • les • tial (suh-**les**-chuhl) *adj*
Of, or relating to, heaven; heavenly

in • vin • ci • ble (in-**vin**-suh-buhl) *adj*
Incapable of being defeated or overcome

min • ion (**min**-yuhn) *noun*
Person who obediently serves or works for a powerful person; Satan's demon

pil • grim (**pil**-gruhm) *noun*
A person who journeys to unfamiliar places

ran • cid (**ran**-sid) *adj*
Having a strong unpleasant smell or taste

roast (rōst) *verb*
To make fun of or criticize someone in either a serious or joking way

scythe (sīth) *noun*
A tool that has a curved blade on a long curved handle; used either as a weapon or to cut grain by hand

shoo-in (shü-in) *noun*
Someone that is a certain and easy winner

sphinx (sfingks) *noun*
An ancient Egyptian imaginary figure having the body of a lion and the head of a man or animal

A real dime piece: Very pretty, beautiful; A perfect ten!

Don't sweat this: Don't worry or be nervous

Get his bearings: Knowing where he is in his surroundings

Hangin' low and lettin' knowledge be born: Staying alone and learning new things

Messin' with my hide: Taking a chance at my body getting hurt

Off the chain: Awesome

Pressin' me: Pressuring or bothering me

Shelby Mustang: A fast high performance sports car built by the Ford Motor Company from 1965–1970

Tripped out: Crazy

Wound up so tight: Uptight; nervous

WORDS AND PHRASES FROM THE STORY I WOULD LIKE TO LEARN ARE:

ALLEGORY WORD CHART

THE MEANING OF PEOPLE AND PLACES IN *CHRISTIAN'S QUEST*

ALLEGORY WORD	MEANING
Allure	Someone who has charm; Is attractive and tempts others to desire him/her
Armor	Invisible protection that God offers to those who belong to Him
Battle	The final Battle of Armageddon where God will defeat evil forever; talked about in the book of Revelation
Blazin'	Someone who is hot, very attractive
Book	The Bible; God's true words; a map that tells us how we should live
Burden	Knowledge of our sin—wrong choices that we have made
Celestial City	Heaven
Charity	Someone who unselfishly loves and helps others
Christian	Someone who believes in Jesus and follows Him
City of Zion	Time right before death when believers are at peace and enjoy the company of family and friends
Cool Crew	A group of people who are comfortable living life their own way—the world thinks is cool, not God's way
Creator	God, who made all things
D'City (City of Destruction)	The world we live in
Dark River	Death; time when a person dies
Dead Man's Swamp/ Slough of Despond	Place of deep discouragement caused by guilt and shame over past wrong choices; when we think we are not good enough to become a Christian or that God won't want us or love us
Discretion	Someone who has great wisdom
Doubting Castle	Place of fear, hopelessness, questioning what we believe
Easy	Someone who has no personal or physical boundaries; never says no to what others want; sleeps around
Evangelist	Someone who tells others about God and His ways
Faith	Someone who has a firm belief, confidence, and trust in God; For All I Trust Him
Faithful	Someone who has a lot of faith (see Faith)
Fortune	Someone who is rich; has lots of money and possessions
Friendly	Someone who shows friendship; is kind, helpful
Giant Despair	Someone who is cruel and enjoys keeping others in deep depression, discouragement, hopelessness
Good Shepherd	Jesus—watching over, leading, and taking care of those who believe in and follow Him
Goodwill	Someone who is accepting and friendly; shows kindness to everyone
Haunted Valley	Place of great hardship, discouragement, uncertainty
Help	A believer in Jesus who rescues, or assists, someone in need
Hill of Difficulty	Place of great struggle
Hope	Someone who wants something and fully expects that it will happen
Hopeful	Someone who has a lot of hope (see Hope)

Allegory Word Chart

ALLEGORY WORD	MEANING
House of the Interpreter	Where things of God and the Bible are explained clearly
Ignorance	Someone having no understanding of the ways of God; thinking he/she can get into heaven just by doing good works, instead of receiving the gift of salvation and grace
Insecurity	Someone who is not confident or sure of themselves; doesn't think they have worth
Interpreter	The Holy Spirit who helps believers understand what God says in His Word
Jovial	Someone who is always happy and encouraging
Judge Haterade	Someone who is very negative, making life hard for those who want to do right—saying hurtful things, putting others down for no reason
Key of Promise	The reminder of God's truths and promises that always come true
King	God
King's Son	Jesus
Light	Jesus and His great brightness; glory
Mistrust	Someone who doesn't have belief or confidence in something/someone
Obstinate	Someone who is stubborn and set in their ways
Palace Beautiful	The Church
Place of the Cross	Calvary; the place where Jesus died for all sins
Pliable	Someone who is a follower; easily influenced or persuaded
Prince	Satan, the devil
River of Life	The life-giving power that only comes from God
Sack	See Burden
Scroll	The assurance of the Holy Spirit; the seal that guarantees a believer is saved and will go to heaven
Self	The inner battle within ourselves; the struggle between living as we want to and submitting totally to God and His ways
Shepherd's Gate	The only way to heaven; believing in Jesus is the only way
Shining Ones	Angels
Shining Ones at the Cross	The Trinity—Father, Son, and Holy Spirit. The Father (God) gives us a new identity and adopts us as His child; the Son (Jesus) frees us completely from our sins; the Holy Spirit gives us the assurance of belonging to God forever
Slough of Despond/ Dead Man's Swamp	See Dead Man's Swamp
Talkative	Someone who says the right things about God, but doesn't live them out; can talk the talk, but doesn't walk the walk
Timorous	Someone who is easily frightened
Truth	Pastor of a church; speaks of God's truths
Valley of Peace	Time when we have hardly any troubles, are happy and content
Vanity Fair	Place where people live opposite of God's ways; live anyway they choose—what feels, sounds, and looks good; they try to tempt and distract believers away from God
Watchful	Someone who is continually aware of other's needs; always on the lookout
Worldly Wise	Someone who is very smart with the ways of the world; smooth talker; tries to distract believers away from following God

ACKNOWLEDGMENTS

Jacqueline would like to thank . . .

Dad and Mom: For introducing me to *Pilgrim's Progress* as a little girl and for showing me the King's way. I owe the beginning of my journey to you both. I love you.

Treasure: The King knew I needed you long before I did. Thank you for answering His call and for patiently and lovingly walking this journey with me, making my long-time dream come true. I'm forever grateful.

My God-given family who have lovingly supported and encouraged me faithfully along the way: **Paul and Margaret, Aunt Doris, the Busch family, Pops and Grams, my C4S team, my Circle Urban family, Parkview sisters, and FB friends** (you know who you are!). My life is richer and more blessed because of you and I thank God for you all.

Tina, Jenn, Tammie, Nicole, and fellow Starbucks baristas: Your friendly encouragement and yummy sugar-free vanilla nonfat chai lattes made writing so much more enjoyable! Thank you.

Melvin would like to thank . . .

Jackie: For having enough faith in me to include me in two of the most rewarding projects of my artistic career.

My children: For being understanding about the time put into this project. Daddy promises to make it up to you, Lord willing.

My mother: For always picking up my many crumpled sheets of paper as I worked to develop my techniques.

Gramps: For being a great example of what it is to be a loving and caring man and for giving me inspiration. Hope you can read this in heaven!

My second grade teacher: For allowing me to find my artistic self.

A special shout-out to **Stephanye Johnson:** I hope I did your girl, Faithful, justice.

Jacqueline and Melvin would like to thank . . .

Lift Every Voice Books Publishers and **Cynthia Ballenger** for believing in these first-time authors and giving us this once-in-a-lifetime opportunity. We are deeply grateful.

Bob Mead: For unselfishly sharing your gifts, experience, and wisdom in assisting with this project. You are a Godspot!

David Augustus: For your quiet, steady, godly influence and encouragement. Thanks, Bro!

ALEC LONDON SERIES

978-0-8024-0411-4
978-0-8024-0410-7
978-0-8024-0412-1
978-0-8024-0414-5
978-0-8024-0413-8

The Alec London books are chapter books written for boys, 8–12 years old. Alec London is introduced in Stephanie Perry Moore's previously released series Morgan Love. In this new series, readers get a glimpse of Alec's life up close and personal. The series provides moral lessons that will aid in character development, teaching boys how to effectively deal with the various issues they face at this stage of life. The books will also help boys develop their English and math skills as they read through the stories and complete the entertaining and educational exercises provided at the end of each chapter and in the back of the book.

Also available as eBooks

L E V B
LIFT EVERY VOICE BOOKS

LiftEveryVoiceBooks.com
MoodyPublishers.com

ALSO RANS SERIES

The Also Rans series is written for boys, ages 8-12. This series enourages youth, especially young boys, to give all they got in everything they do and never give up.

978-0-8024-2253-8

RUN, JEREMIAH, RUN

As a foster child, life for Jeremiah is a garbage bag filled with his things, a new school, and worst of all, finding a new family. Jeremiah holds on to his grandmother's promise of a handful of mustard seeds being planted one day to grow into a tree of his own. After being expelled from school again, he thinks that no one will want him to be a part of their family. With the help of his friends, he learns about teamwork and what it means to persevere.

978-0-8024-2259-0

COMING ACROSS JORDAN

When Jordan and brother Kevin decide to paint a mural (which is really graffiti) on the school's property, they get in trouble. They learn, along with their good friend Melanie, the lesson that even in using their talents to do something good, they have to pay attention and not break the rules.

Also available as eBooks

L E V B
LIFT EVERY VOICE BOOKS

LiftEveryVoiceBooks.com
MoodyPublishers.com